Fire from the Ashes: Rose River Romance Book 1

A Small Town Cowboy Romance

Avery Lawrence

SR Endeavors LLC Publishing

Chapter One

D ense smoke curled upward, blocking the sun and obscuring the tree line. Logan's swift movements only added to the confusion of the skittish horses. Their wild eyes darted between him and the encroaching danger, their hooves pawing at the dirt. Only two had escalated into anxious bucks attacking the edges of the corral. Logan threw up the latch like he was popping the top on a soda and pushed open the gate. Drifter was out before the gate had fully opened and others followed. Daisy hung back, frozen at the entrance to the barn, unsure which direction to go.

Logan swung himself up over the edge of the fence and into the corral, steering clear of the other frantically escaping horses. He approached Daisy tentatively with his hands open in front of him. He sucked air in slowly, trying to modulate the pace of his heart—knowing Daisy would sense any sign of fear. He felt his phone vibrate in his back pocket, and while he was glad it was on silent, it added to the tension. His head gave a slight shake. It was likely his mom. Although she had no clue what was going on, for once she couldn't argue that her call, and likely an attempt to force him on a blind date, was more important.

"Come on, girl," he moved to the left and expanded his right arm towards the open gate, "just follow your friends. It's safer out there."

Daisy's eyes danced from the smoke to the gate and back to Logan.

"Trust me, Daisy. I've never steered you wrong; *go*."

Daisy shook her mane in defiance and dug her front hooves into the ground.

A hopeful breath caught in Logan's chest as he saw the ripple of her muscles tensing for movement. Her head leaned to the left —

And she swiftly turned tail and ran into the barn.

Logan took his hat off and threw it on the ground. The straw brim was still stiff, but it was laced with sweat and showing wear. He hoped Tony and Nate were more successful in letting the other animals loose. He quickened his pace towards the barn and pivoted as Boots barked his arrival.

"Boots—get out of here. This isn't safe." Boots ran into the corral and to his side, as though hearing her name meant this was where she needed to be. Logan reached down to give her a quick pat and then shooed her away.

"Really, Boots, go help with the cows. Get out of here." He flicked his wrists towards the gate.

Boots didn't move. Logan gave her a little push, mumbling pointless pleas under his breath.

A loud whinny from Daisy snapped his attention.

The back of the barn crackled as it ignited with flames.

He ran to the door, yelling for her.

Daisy was backed into a stall; manically thrashing against the walls, releasing loud whinnies. He climbed the wall of the stall next to hers, swatting at her backside, hoping to move her towards the door. The words he hurled at her were of no use, her panic and the crackling flames fully eclipsed them.

His stomach churned with the realization that he needed to get in there with her. He grabbed a rope off the wall and since there wasn't enough space to lasso; he fashioned a knot that would tighten if he could just get it around her neck.

Boots nipped at his heels as though Logan didn't understand the imminent danger they were all in. "Boots—focus. Daisy—not me."

He took a momentary pause. Boots knew this was a bad idea as well. His mind reeled, searching for other options.

There were none.

He entered the stall with the crazed creature; no longer his sweet and calm Daisy.

He kept his hands where she could see them, but her eyes couldn't even focus. She continued to buck and twist in anguish. "Daisy—Daisy—Calm down, girl." He reached his arm towards her neck—offering a soothing touch. His fingers almost brushed her mane when she ripped her head away. Her snout came so close that he backed slightly out of the stall. He moved in again—bobbing around her erratic movements. Trying to find a path.

With a lightning quick reflex, he lunged in, grabbing her neck. He deftly slid the rope over her ears. Before he could drop it the length of her face—Daisy flung all of her weight into him. Logan found himself half on the floor and half against the wall, with the rope nowhere in sight.

He was running out of options. The flames were eating the sun-parched wood of the barn at a rapid rate. He stood up and contorted himself at a right angle to swat her flank. Her front hooves bucked up with a squeal and landed sharply. Holding her position in this small space.

Logan ran to the pen next to her, deftly climbing the fence. He stood on the rail balancing himself with the two fingers that could reach the beam overhead. Daisy's eyes flitted between him and the flames, her ears pinned flat, nostrils flared.

"Boots!" Boots turned attentively to Logan. "Get Daisy."

Boots ran in to nip at Daisy's feet. As soon as her head lowered, Logan raised his brows and whispered, "Here goes nothing."

He brought his arm down to balance himself briefly and jumped.

He landed squarely on the back of the mare. His arms wrapped around her neck, expecting a potential buck.

Daisy threw her head back in surprise. She didn't have enough momentum to lift her legs before Logan's heels hit the right spot and she propelled forward, nearly knocking over Boots. Logan raised himself slightly, taking a handful of Daisy's mane and using his weight shifted her towards the exit of the barn.

Logan's eyes shot up in response to a loud crack overhead. The rafter splintered in flames and a section close to the door broke loose. He pulled back on Daisy as they neared the door. Daisy's front legs lifted off the ground and Logan leaned in. She skittered on her back legs before dropping her front hooves, rearing back once more; bolting towards the door. Logan's grip slipped somewhere between the second drop and her bolt.

Things shifted to slow motion.

Boots loving woof, Daisy safely clearing the barn door without a glance back. The weightless sensation of his body in flight. The spicy acrid fumes oppressing him and the thundering crackle devouring the sum total of all he cared about.

His head slowly rotated to assess where and how he might land, but a jolt of pain seared through him and everything went black.

———ℓℓℓ———

"**P**rop him up, prop him up." Nate threw the words over his shoulder through the small opening that separated the cab of the truck from the bed.

Tony didn't hear a word of it. The sirens canceled all noise, taking claim to the air, pushing back against the smoke. Tony didn't even lift his head at the powerful cavalry in large red trucks careening towards the raging blaze.

A grimy mix of soot, dirt, and sweat streaked what was visible of Tony's skin, broken by jagged scratches and thin streaks of blood. His face was expressionless, and his attention focused on Logan. The cloudiness in his eyes was his cousin's voice echoing in his mind, Dr. Morales, chastising him even before they made it to the clinic.

You never move someone after a fall. He could have broken his neck.

Tony wasn't the one to move him. Nate had pulled Logan from the barn, and Tony just helped lift him to the bed of the truck. It wouldn't matter, though. If there was any permanent damage done to Logan, he would never forgive himself.

They'd been careful. Horse blankets grabbed from the porch rail lined the truck bed and they placed another under him to assure they lifted him gently. Dr. Morales' voice didn't care,

You should have waited for the ambulance; he needed stretchers, braces, professionals.

There was a case to be made that with the thirsty conditions and the speed of the wildfire, the ambulance may never have made it up the mountain in time. Even if they did, that barn crashed down not long after Tony pulled Logan's unconscious body out.

Drastic measures were the only option.

Kneeling next to Logan, cradling his head to hold it steady; there wasn't room for those facts. Tony's shoulders slumped with guilt and worry. His eyes were eagle sharp as he diligently watched for any signs of movement, and his lips moved almost imperceptibly as the prayers tumbled out.

Chapter Two

I zzy's fingers worked frantically to remove the smudge of ketchup from the front of her blouse. This is what happens when you eat in the car. *You know better.* Glancing at the clock on her dash, she dropped her shoulders in an exhale. She was seven minutes late, and even though she was technically in charge, she still felt she couldn't get away with it.

Pawing around the backseat, she found a scarf with a reasonable pattern and decided she would pretend the AC made her cold. Grabbing her purse, she rushed in the door.

She chastised herself again for leaving Marco's lunch in the car this morning. It was incredibly embarrassing to have the school call to remind you to feed your kid. In addition, it was also impossible to get to his preschool and back to the clinic in the short half-hour she had for lunch. No one at work understood either. How was it possible that she was the only person at the clinic who had a young kid? That's what happens when half the staff is docs and (in a small town) they are all fresh out of their residency rotations and medical school. The Social Worker was also here fresh out of graduate school looking for loan forgiveness, and the Medical Assistant (MA) well, not to judge, but it's for the best that she doesn't have kids. Betsy in Accounting and the nurse Raya were both grandmas. This meant they had an ounce of empathy, but they mostly didn't think you should work when your kids were young. That only left Fred at the front desk, and he didn't really have a reason. Maybe it's just hard to meet people in a small town?

Izzy had only been back in Rose River for less than a year. She never imagined coming back here, especially after spending almost seven years in LA, but here she was. Being a single mom is a lot easier when you have family around and the cost of living was a lot more affordable on the Oregon Coast than anywhere in California. So, when there was a job that matched her degree and her experience, how could she say no?

"Well, isn't it sweet of you to join us?" Kit's sarcasm was so thick you could almost see it dripping from her lips.

Izzy managed a small smile, tried to raise her head a little more, and continued the walk to her office. She didn't answer to the MA- the MA answered to her. Even if the MA could make her look bad in front of the patients and anyone else within earshot.

Just don't engage.

Placing her purse on the hook by the door, she almost took the scarf off out of habit, before remembering she placed it there for a reason. She inhaled deeply as she circled to her desk to tackle the budget forecasting and approve orders.

"Don't let her get to you." Dr. Carrington's tone was conspiratorial when he peeked his head into her office. His dusky hair looked darker when it was freshly cut, and his green eyes danced a little behind his wire-rimmed glasses. He had a wise, fatherly look about him, even if he wasn't much older than Izzy. It constantly begged the question- does he look that way *because* he is a doctor, or would he still have that vibe if he was a plumber?

"What, Kit? She's secretly my biggest fan."

He raised his eyebrows, calling her bluff.

A grin crept across Izzy's face as she continued, "It is such a good secret, she doesn't even know it yet."

"You'll have to let me know when she figures it out. That'll be a sight to see."

"Don't hold your breath," Izzy assured him.

"Didn't you guys go to high school together or something?"

"She was my brother's age—dated his best friend back in the day. She's like 3 or 4 years older than me. I hardly remember her or that time." Izzy waved it off. "I've lived at least two lives since then."

"Well, if you ever need anyone to fire her, I've got your back," Dr. Carrington said.

Izzy squinted at him slightly, trying to gauge his seriousness, and tentatively responded, "I'll keep that in mind."

With a simple wave, Dr. Carrington backed away from the door. Kit interrupted his departure, yelling his name down the hall. Dr. Carrington and Izzy exchanged a look. Maybe this was the offense warranting firing? Who yells like that at a Medical Clinic?

Izzy followed Dr. Carrington and even her brother, Dr. Morales, had come out of his exam room to address the commotion.

"What is going on? I'm with a patient."

"We'll figure it out, sorry." Izzy shrugged and walked faster.

Kit had already exited into the lobby and as Izzy and Dr. Carrington did the same, Kit was already out the front doors. Their feet were catching on the carpet as they chose between quickening steps and looking at each other to sort their confusion.

When the second set of automatic doors parted, Izzy could make out her cousin Tony's truck at the center of the uproar. In two more steps, she clutched her stomach. Her hand flew to her mouth as her chest caved in. "Logan." His name left her lips as a whispered gasp. Ice poured into her veins.

Everyone from the office was out there, mouths agape, trying to comprehend the limp body, the soot, sweat, traces of blood, and Tony delicately holding Logan's head in place. She turned to Betsy. "Go get my brother, Andres. He's in exam room 2."

Chapter Three

T he rhythmic ache pulsing through his head was the first thing Logan felt. Before he could open his eyes, there was a jolt of pain through his right arm that bit into his shoulder. The surrounding din made it hard to assess where he was. His eyes squinted tighter as he fought to pry them open.

"We have to transfer him. We can't assess him fully here." The man's voice was commanding and raised above the others.

"Do we need an ambulance? Is his condition critical enough to warrant that?" The woman's voice was soft and unfamiliar. He channeled his energy to open his eyes. His eyelashes kept flittering—obscuring his vision.

"Oh, my gosh. Did you see that?" This was a voice he definitely recognized. Sometimes a little rushed, just like her brother, but it still wrapped you like a warm blanket. "He just moved his eyes."

All the other voices chimed in, and he could no longer distinguish one over another. He instinctively shifted into a slight twist, pulling himself towards sitting. He hadn't made it an inch off the table before hands on either shoulder pressed him back down.

"Not so fast. Just because you can open your eyes doesn't mean you need to be moving around." As Andres said the words, he leaned towards the bed's controls, positioning Logan to be better elevated as the weight in his belly absorbed the large audience. Logan sucked in a deep breath to soothe himself. Instead, it seemed to awaken fire ants of pain.

Andres had been Logan's best friend since they first took over the tether ball court in first grade. Throughout the years, even after Andres went off to medical school, that initial connection of their lone wolf competitive spirits continued to grow; no matter how different they seemed with just an outside glance.

Andres took one scan of Logan's eyes and before he even pulled out the light to do his medical duty, he performed his duty as a friend.

"OK, Everyone out. We don't need this much chaos. There needs to be room to evaluate our patient."

Logan's ex-girlfriend Kit was a medical assistant at the clinic, though she always made it sound like she was a highly respected nurse. She was the closest to the door and the most - reticent to leave. Izzy, Andres' younger sister, was next to her, and literally using her hands to nudge Kit out of the room. This image curled one side of Logan's lips into a partial smile, revealing his dimple, and gave a momentary distraction from assessing all the places the pain radiated from.

Kit's hair was still in perfect amber waves, a contrast to the streaks of black streaming from her watery eyes and smudged across her cheeks. She'd twisted her lips in anguish, her long slender body still angling for the room, and her white knuckles proving her grip on the doorjamb. Next to her, with hands pressing firmly against Kit's upper hip, was sweet patient Izzy. She was at least a foot shorter, her ebony hair in a messy bun, her pale brown eyes laser-focused on the task at hand, her face and form perfectly composed, undeterrable.

Waiting behind Izzy, as though she was next in line for the cashier, was a woman Logan had yet to meet and the owner of the mysterious voice from earlier. Willa Jones had only arrived in Rose River a few months prior when the clinic received a grant from the Empowering Rural Medicine Project, which included hiring their first social worker. Willa was fresh out of graduate school and had come from the other side of the country. She looked a little lost, as though she was constantly standing in lines, and never knew what was on the other side.

"Actually, Dr. Morales," Dr. Carrington was one of the few people who consistently called Andres Dr. Morales. Coming back to practice in your hometown meant you could never simply be who you are; you would always be who they knew you as, something Andres had a hard time with. "My recommendation is still that he needs to be taken to Junction Valley. If he would rather I do more to see if I can treat him here, *you* should leave me to my work as well."

Sometimes Andres appreciated the big city/alternate perspective that Dr. Carrington brought to the table. This was not one of those times. The exodus from the room had paused and everyone seemed to wait on Andres' response.

Logan steadied his focus and forced himself to form words, even though they were stilted. "I don't want to cause trouble. I'll just drive myself up..." Logan had made the mistake of shifting his weight towards sitting as he spoke. This time, no one moved quick enough to stop him. It felt like someone had jettisoned down a wrecking ball and it was swinging forward, searing through his thoughts like they were loose webs, and leaving a deep blurring ache in its wake. Words were no longer something he could access.

He'd already laid himself back down when Dr. Carrington was at his side speaking delicately to him, "Logan, my name is Dr. Carrington. Your friends brought you to this clinic because you have several injuries as a result of a fall. I am still evaluating you, but the wound on your head suggests, at the very least, a severe concussion. You have several abrasions and potentially broken bones and other tissue damage. We can continue to assess you here, and probably get you a little better stabilized, but I would recommend getting a full work up at Junction Valley Hospital."

Thoughts were rolling around in Logan's head like the spiky seeds from a chestnut tree. He knew he needed to answer or they may call up an ambulance he really couldn't afford.

"Yeah," he paused and moved his tongue around, suddenly realizing how thirsty he was and recognizing the gritty soot on his lips. "Junction's good, I'll go. Um..." his chest heaved in a cough. He instinctively lifted his right hand and winced in tandem with the jolt of agony that told him he may have located one of the broken bones they mentioned.

"Do you want to go straightaway? We can have the front desk call the ambulance for you, or we can stabilize you a little further first." Dr. Carrington was bent towards Logan, a slight shielding from the entourage who, other than Kit, had evaded the requested exit.

"Um, no," were all the words that Logan could muster as he let his eyelids shroud some of the light.

The low tone of Andres' voice conveyed the importance and delicate nature of the words he was sharing. "Logan runs a ranch. He has catastrophe insurance, but an ambulance ride transporting him to the hospital probably isn't something they cover. Growing up in this town, we are all well aware of the staggering bill you get after taking that long ride to Junction City."

Dr. Carrington released a deep breath. There were some things he loved about this little town, but the distance of the nearest large-scale medical facility was probably the greatest challenge. He was vaguely aware of how the ambulances gouged folks in LA, but they didn't have their captors for long. He glanced down at Logan and back up at Dr. Morales. He had already noted that the computerized chart listed Dr. Morales as Logan Robert's emergency contact, and that the documentation giving Dr. Morales Power of Attorney for Medical Directives was on file. That was the biggest reason he was kicking Dr. Morales out of the room. He shouldn't be providing medical care. However, for decisions about Logan's care when Logan was still in a delicate state, Dr. Morales was the right person to have there.

"How else do we suggest we get him there?"

Dr. Morales had this answer ready. "I'll take him. I just need to clear my schedule."

Izzy quickly jumped in, "Andres, you are already an hour behind because of this. You still have a patient waiting. You're our only Spanish-speaking physician and people book weeks in advance to see you. Don't make them reschedule for 3 weeks from now."

Andres' first instinct was to correct her—Dr. Morales. When she referred to his work as a physician, she should call him that. She had a point, though, and now was not the time.

"How about you Willa? Your schedule isn't full yet, and this falls loosely under the social support realm." Andres turned to her suddenly and his eyes were wide with expectation.

Willa's face flushed crimson. He had never asked anything of her. She didn't want her first answer to be no. How could she disappoint him? She pulled at her wrist and dug her toe into the ground. "I'm so sorry," she staggered her words, "I have a friend arriving this weekend. I—I have so much to do to prepare—"

"I shouldn't have asked." The tips of his ears reddened as Andres turned back towards

Logan. It was as though he was checking to make sure they didn't both feel that rejection.

Izzy's voice sliced through the awkwardness. "I'll take him. You have patients, you have plans. I can make up my administrative work over the weekend." Andres' eyes traced a line between Izzy and Logan, bouncing back and forth.

"What about Marco? You won't be back in time for when he gets off school."

Izzy pursed her lips. "I moved here because I have family here. I am sure mom or Selena can pick him up."

Dr. Carrington saw the situation as resolved. "Just don't let those sly doctors at Junction Valley lure you away from us, Izzy. Hopefully, you find that there are more reasons than family that make you want to stay. Now, all of you—*out*. Send in Raya. She is probably the only person who should have been here in the first place."

"Sorry about that, Dr. Carrington. I was making quick decisions and thought I should have the nurse stay with Dr. Morales' patient as he headed to tend with the arriving emergency.

I should have shuffled things sooner." She winced as the words tumbled out of her mouth. She had responded to this entire situation as a close friend of the injured, vs. the Director of the Medical Clinic. She also realized she may have called her brother by his first name. Hopefully, none of this made it back to the hospital board. *She needed to do better.*

Logan tracked pieces of the conversation, but it was like he lost some words to a bad cell signal. He was merely a confused observer in this dance of decision making.

He liked it when Izzy spoke. Her voice always cut through. Once, when they were young, the guys had all fallen asleep in tents in the Morales' yard. Logan was restless. He got up and walked around the property. A lump on the ground perplexed him when he was walking near the pasture. As he got closer, it transformed into a silhouette, and then into Izzy whispering to herself, the names of constellations, as he would later learn. It was the first time he had genuinely heard her voice. It was the first time he had been with just her. It was outside her bustling family, away from the obnoxious group of guys. The first time he really saw her was in the dark. Maybe that was why her voice could still cut through the murkiness.

Chapter Four

I zzy's fingers traced the outline of the steering wheel at every stoplight. She still wasn't clear about her role. Did she talk to him? Did she let him rest? They had said she need to make sure he could talk every half hour, but she didn't want to engage him in unnecessary conversation if he needed to rest. Logan twisted slightly in the seat; jeans rubbing against leather.

"I'm sorry I'm such terrible company." He half mumbled the words, his eyes barely open.

"I don't think this drive is really about you keeping me company." Her heart swelled in her chest every time she glanced at him. She wasn't sure if it was her motherly instinct kicking in and concern over his wellbeing, or a trace of something else. It might be more than the dust and the wounds and the well of concern. Her eyes traced the strong line of his jaw, the dimple in his left cheek that remained even when his smile faded.

"I doubt driving up to Junction City was at the top of your plans today. The least I could be is decent company."

"It was the perfect excuse to escape the office. I love doing my work over the weekends; it makes me feel less guilty about not having a social life." Her lips spread in a small smile. There was more truth in her words than she intended.

Her words were met with silence, and she let her mind drift. It was still surreal to be back in Rose River. Everything was so different here.

She didn't miss the traffic of LA, but the slow pace of Rose River had been the pace of her childhood. Now that she was 26, it felt like she'd passed through the looking glass and it was all a touch distorted. She flipped on her windshield wipers in response to a light mist. Another thing she rarely saw in LA.

"I don't believe that." Logan's words caught her off guard, and Izzy inhaled a small laugh.

"I thought you'd dozed off."

"Hey, it just takes me a minute to process things. Must be the painkillers." His voice was modulated and low, his words required effort.

"That's definitely it," she responded. "I'm sure being bucked off a horse after trying to save everything you love from a raging wildfire and slamming your head into the ground has nothing to do with it."

"Hey, now..." His eyes were sharp, but the slight curl to his lips meant he was accepting her chiding. She raised her hands in surrender. She shouldn't torture her patient too much. Izzy wasn't used to him like this. He was always closed off and quiet. His watchful eyes always seemed to take things in, and today they seemed to let things seep out. She might enjoy the fluidity the painkillers were bringing to the mix.

"I think you should be resting. You can let the gorgeous pine trees and the occasional view of the ocean entertain me, and you can focus on healing."

Logan's chortle took her by surprise. "Yep, an hour of quiet ought to heal me right up."

"Now that's the Logan I know—sarcastic." She glanced back at him. "Obviously, you've got more than an hour ahead of you for healing. So, I guess you'd better get used to a little less worrying about everything else and a little more about resting and taking care of yourself."

Logan examined Izzy's profile, the soft curve to her cheeks, her cute impish nose, and the erratic bun that begged to be loosened so her hair could fall to her shoulders. He soaked in her words. Was this just something she would say to anybody? Or did she see that in him? Did she get he was the one taking care of everyone?

How could she know the ranch depended on him?

After his father died, he was the one that had to run it all.

He was nineteen at the time and the only reason they could keep the land and all the animals. His mom had some sort of crisis and mutated into a socialite who moved to the far-off city. His brother went on with college and then started a family. He was the one holding it together. He was the one with the ledgers and the contracts, the farm hands to pay, the business to learn, and his mom's evolved lifestyle to support.

At least he did. Today it all turned to ashes.

"Hey, everything okay?" Izzy's voice broke through the silence and snapped Logan back to the moment.

He glanced down at his body- the splint immobilizing his arm, the dirt and ash that thickly lined the places the nurse had cleared and cleaned. It impressed him how well the pain medication worked. It removed the sharp edge and made it so he knew it was still there, but it didn't take up space in his thoughts or awareness.

"Yep, dandy. I don't even think they were right about this arm being broken."

"They took x-rays, Logan. You broke your wrist. They just weren't sure if it would need a surgical pin. It's one reason we are going to the hospital, remember?" She waited for him to give a small nod. "But that look in your eyes was what I was asking about, not your list of injuries. I know that body is not okay, but I also know you'll heal up just fine. You're resilient."

"Oh, yeah, I'm good. Just a little loopy, I guess. Must be that concussion you were talking about."

Logan rolled his head away from her to look at the window and watch the trees and broken bits of mountain whiz past. He needed to be careful with this one. She saw more than he realized.

Izzy's tooth bit into her bottom lip, and she reluctantly looked back at the road. She knew better than to try. This is how guys were, right? They acted like everything was fine when it was so obvious that it wasn't. Not her problem, though. This was just her brother's best friend. Thank goodness she wasn't dating him. She had enough of dealing with guys that didn't know how to communicate when she was with Marco's dad. She'd gladly left that behind.

Chapter Five

"You are going to need to stay with him for the next 24 hours. He needs rest and should sleep, but you'll have to wake him up every 2-3 hours and ask him some basic—"

"She won't be staying with me," Logan spoke over the top of the doctor. "I'm fine on my own." Logan's assertion for independence became more adamant as the painkillers from the clinic wore off.

"I didn't mean to assume, but someone needs to stay with you." The doctor's eyes floated back and forth between the two of them, not sure where they should land.

A sharp breath escaped as Izzy's eyes flitted into a roll. "Logan, don't be ridiculous. I'll stay with you." The second she said the words, she realized they didn't know if his place was somewhere that anyone could stay. "Or, umm—you can stay with me, or umm—we'll stay at Andres' house."

Logan's face stayed turned downward. The slight movement of his eyes was the only indication that he was considering any of what they were saying.

He pressed back against the stack of pillows the nurse had left him.

"Is it really necessary? I seem to be bandaged up just fine—I can manage."

"It isn't about the bandages, Logan. We know you hit your head, and it is hard to know the extent of the injury simply from our scans. Things can develop over time. We need someone to wake you up every few hours and make sure you can process information. It is necessary to know that things aren't deteriorating." The doctor paused, hoping what he shared was enough. "The only other option is to stay here in the hospital."

Logan's chest rose and fell with an audible sigh.

He closed his eyes and stretched his chin towards the ceiling.

Izzy's arms wrapped around her chest, her thumb and forefinger twiddling a lock of hair.

"I'll come back by in a bit, but I can't sign release papers until I have a signed plan for your aftercare." The doctor ruffled his fingers through his thick dark hair, evened out the ends of his stethoscope, and nodded to Izzy as he walked out of the room.

Izzy didn't know what to say. Logan was stubborn, and she wasn't about to supplicate him with offers of help. She also knew they weren't leaving until he agreed. Shuffling her feet, she moved closer to the wall and simply leaned into it. This was going to take a while.

Logan still had his eyes closed and head tilted back. The heaviness of each breath clarified that he was very much conscious and trying to process the options before him. *He didn't need help.* It made no sense. There had to be an option they hadn't considered. He could set an alarm and call into the hospital at set intervals. Maybe that would work?

He popped his head up and met Izzy's eyes before moaning and lowering his head slowly back to the side. Izzy rushed to him, pulling the pillows to meet his head and preventing him from straining further.

"You can't even lift your head up and yet you seem to think you can handle this all on your own." Her voice was soft and firm, gently correcting a child rather than using sass to put him in line. He could tell the difference and much preferred the sass.

He couldn't argue, though. Even with his eyes clenched tight, the room was still wobbling around him and the churn it was causing in his gut meant opening his mouth was a game of Russian Roulette. He blamed it on the painkillers. Those things were not meant to be taken on an empty stomach and food had sounded completely unappealing to him. He sensed Izzy moving away from him and instinctively reached his hand out to the place he last heard her. It was a mere moment before she gently touched his fingers.

"I got you a cold rag. Hopefully, it will help. I don't want to get your bandage wet, so I am going to get it on the back of your neck." Her fingers lingered a moment longer against his before she took them to smooth back his sandy blond strands from the nape of his neck and laid the cool cloth against the skin that was easily accessible.

He breathed in the shock of the cold and brought his hand to cradle his forehead and shield his eyes. Maybe it would help if he opened them. Even with his hand blocking the light, he had to blink numerous times. It surprised him how something as simple as raising his head quickly set things off. The coolness on his neck seemed to short circuit some of it. He still felt lightheaded, and his stomach still roiled, but the room had settled to an almost imperceptible sway. He'd felt better on the drive here, but after the moving around for scans, exams, and what not; his body was in full-out protest.

The fluorescent lights seemed to cast a glow around Izzy. It contrasted her ebony hair and accentuated its soft waves as it fell over her shoulders. She'd finally let it down. The angle of the light made it hard to see her eyes, but he could feel them emitting warmth. She held the cool rag in place with one hand and used the other to smooth the unruly wisps of his hair that peeked out from under the bandages and flipped away from his forehead in defiance.

"It's twenty-four hours, Logan. Probably from the time of the accident, so I could be gone by lunch. It won't be that bad."

She leaned towards him and abruptly stopped herself. She was about to kiss his forehead. *Where did that come from?* It must've been a nurture reflex that she hadn't experienced outside of her son before. This was the first time she'd been on the side of a hospital bed since her father had passed years earlier.

She pulled the cloth away and smoothed her hair as she walked the rag to the sink.

"I'll give you some space to think."

She left before Logan could answer and without looking back.

Chapter Six

T he halls were emptier now. She looked at her phone and realized it was almost 8:30 p.m., she might need to make her way to the cafeteria and find some food before they closed. Everything had taken so long, and yet the minutes had flown by.

The cafeteria held the aroma of baking bread. She guessed they were baking for the morning because nothing she saw out looked fresh. She settled on a sandwich wrapped in cellophane and walked over to the salad bar to throw something together. As she was settling into the hard plastic chair, she felt the buzzing of her cell phone from her purse. She reached in and pulled it out, noticing her mother's name flashing across the screen. It would be nice to hear a familiar voice.

"Hey, mom. How's Marco doing? Did you get him down to bed already?"

"Yeah, he was out like a light. Sounds like he had a busy day at school, something about an extra recess." Elena loved having her only grandson living close again and her voice sounded like early spring whenever she talked about him.

"That's always a plus. How are things going otherwise?" Izzy tugged at the corner of the cellophane wrapping of her sandwich, frustrated that one hand wasn't enough to get it to budge.

"Let's not worry about me. How are things going with you? How is Logan?" Hearing Elena's voice was like settling into your favorite reading chair and Izzy exhaled a deep breath.

"Well, he definitely looks the worst I've ever seen him." She set down the sandwich and stared off at the geometric pattern on the walls. "But it seems he'll be just fine. He has a distal wrist fracture or something like that. And a concussion. Other than that, it's mostly abrasions and nasty looking wounds from where he hit the ground. They aren't too worried about smoke inhalation since he was so low, and they got him away from the fire so fast." She looked back at her food and poked at her salad with the fork. "I don't know if he's even had time to process what's happened, though. I'm guessing that'll take a while."

"I'm sure. Sounds like it is a mess up there. The good news is that the fire completely spared the house. It sounded like they got it out pretty quickly after he and the boys left. The rain also picked up and helped them get things under control. The fire is still raging another 5-10 minutes down the road, but it's turned away from his place and away from town."

Izzy felt her body relax; she hadn't realized how tense her shoulders were. "That's definitely a relief. It's good to know that his place is okay."

"Yeah, Andres talked to Nate, who got up there to check if any of the animals came back and fed Boots."

Izzy hadn't even thought about Boots. She wondered if Logan's thoughts were clear enough to think about her. He probably had. His mind was probably swirling with a million things he needed to worry about. At least his house was okay.

"Well, it looks like I need to stay with him tonight. However, he's not accepting that option."

Elena laughed slightly, "That sounds like the Logan we all know and love."

Izzy's face lifted slightly at her mom's comment. Maybe it had nothing to do with her. "Is it possible for you to take Marco to school tomorrow?"

"Izzy—he's already at my house. I pretty much figured I was taking him to school tomorrow."

Izzy shook her head slightly. "I'm glad to know you've got him. Thank you, mom."

"Hey, that's what family is for. I'm just glad you're close enough we can finally help like this." Elena paused a beat. "And Logan is pretty lucky that you were there to help him out, too."

"If he'll let me help." Izzy sucked air in through her teeth. "It might be a fight. There's a chance he'll stay at the hospital versus letting me take him home."

Elena let out a low laugh. "You've known Logan most of your life. It shouldn't surprise you he's being stubborn. He's a good guy—doesn't mean he's not a difficult one."

"Yeah, I guess the two aren't mutually exclusive." Izzy shifted in her seat. "I'm gonna eat my questionable-looking salad, possibly this sandwich, and then go back to see if he's made up his mind. I'll try to send you a text when I get to his place or when I leave here to head to mine. Would you let Andres know I won't be in the office tomorrow morning? I'll either start the day from my place or Logan's. I'll call the office in the morning to check-in."

"Sure, I'll let him know. I'm sure he'll be glad to know that Logan's stabilized and should come home tonight. I think a lot of people will be glad to hear that."

"Yeah, thanks for spreading the word. I haven't had time for more than a couple of texts to Andres." Izzy's stomach rumbled and she gathered items from her salad onto the fork.

"I'm sure you're exhausted. It's been quite a day for all of us."

"Yeah, thanks again, mom. I really appreciate you. Love you."

"Love you, too. Bye."

Izzy tucked the phone back into her purse. She was grateful once again for being so close to home. Even if comparing the two wasn't apples to apples. It may be unlikely she'd be the person helping in a situation like this in LA, but having a safe, loving place for her son when things got complicated meant a lot. It was nice to feel supported. Rose River was showing its benefits.

She made her way back to the room slowly. She wasn't sure if Logan would be asleep, still mulling over his decisions, or just unhappy to see her.

When she rounded the corner to his room, it surprised her to see the bed elevated further and him watching the door—like he was waiting for her return.

"You look a little more chipper than the last time I saw you." Izzy tucked her arms behind her as she entered.

"I don't know if I'd go as far as chipper." He said with a slight laugh.

"I guess that might be taking things a little too far. You do look a little better."

"Yeah, they gave me something different. It makes me a little less fuzzy. Which is nice. It's hard to know what's painkillers, and what's the bump on my head. And what's the general overwhelm from the day."

"I bet." Izzy moved to the edge of his bed and smoothed the sheets near his feet. "I have some good news around some of that. I just talked to my mom. She said that the fire has died down a touch and never even touched your house.

It was headed away from town and away from your place. Which is definitely a blessing."

"Wow, I still have a place for it to head away from. Didn't look like there was gonna be much left last time I saw anything." There was a smile creasing Logan's lips, but his eyes were downcast at the blanket near his arm brace.

"It sounds like it completely spared your house. I didn't ask about the other buildings. I don't think she knew much. Sounds like Nate might know more?"

"When I was last there and conscious, we'd lost the barn. I don't know if it spared some of the other outbuildings. I guess we'll find out." His eyes glassed over as he stared off. Trying to picture the property as it once was, and make sense of how it might be now.

She tried to wipe the pity from her face. She knew he wouldn't want to see it.

"So, are you finally willing to surrender and let me drive you home?"

"It depends. Do you promise to make me pancakes?"

A quick bite of laughter escaped from Izzy's throat.

"I don't know that I'm the best at making pancakes. But in this unique case, I think I could definitely try. *If* you're willing to put up with me waking you up every few hours and promise to be nice to me in the process."

"The doc said nothing about needing to be nice to you." Logan hardened his eyes.

"I guess he didn't. Did he?" Izzy raised one eyebrow.

"Yeah," Logan settled his shoulders in slightly. "Sorry about being stubborn. I guess I'm not one for accepting help. I'm usually the one doing things for people."

"Yeah, I kind of see that. I kind of get it too. I'll try not to hold it over your head for too long."

"Don't go do me any favors." Logan's dimple returned. "You're already doing enough of them."

"Now that you've given me permission, I'll remind you that you're headstrong as a mule every chance I get."

"I guess there has to be something about getting out of this hospital that's a negative. Let's get that paperwork."

Chapter Seven

Boots bounced like her legs were on Pogo sticks. She was running from one end of the porch to the other with her tongue hanging out the side of her mouth. At the sight of his beloved pup, Logan's eyes lit up. It was the highlight of everyone's day. As soon as Izzy eased the car into park, Boots was 6 inches from the door. Her paws stretched out and her head lowered. Ready to pounce as soon as Logan opened the door.

It impressed Izzy that Boots had so much self-control. Every dog she'd known would've been scratching at the side of the car by now.

Logan emanated with pride. "Boots is such a good girl. She listens." He reached over to open the car door.

Izzy's breath caught in her chest, trying to decide if she should offer to help. Instead, she reached around, urgently grabbed her purse, and hurried around the car to the passenger side door. She figured the best plan was to be there in case needed, rather than offer anything.

Logan had taken off his seat belt and eased the door open just enough for Boots to stick her head inside. She was nuzzling his leg, and he was curling down towards her, roughing up her fur with his left hand while protectively holding his right arm up in the air. It wasn't clear if he was protecting her from it, or it from her.

Izzy couldn't make out what he was saying to Boots. But whatever it was, it was bringing further joy to that happy pup. She pulled the door open a little further. To make it easier for him to get out once he was ready. She thought it may be a while.

After both had settled slightly, Logan lifted his head and started taking in the surrounding sights. She thought it was interesting he hadn't tried to peer through the darkness and look at the damage to his barn and property. Perhaps he needed Boots by his side before he was willing to soak it all in.

His fingers wrapped in her long fur and flattened before he pulled them tight again. His eyes turned towards the destruction, but they were unflinching. She wondered if he was taking any of it in. He may be at capacity for the day. Boots shifted her head and looked in the same direction, as if she needed to process what they have been through as well.

Izzy shifted her body slightly to move between the two of them and obscure the view of the charred skeleton.

"Hey, it's late. Why don't we get inside and get you settled in?"

Logan's head tilted towards her, and his pupils adjusted to focus. He gave a simple nod and drew in a hard breath.

She knew he could stand on his own. But she also knew they told her to stay close to him in case he stumbled. They had wheeled him out of the hospital in a wheelchair. She knew it was standard hospital protocol, but she also knew he had spent little time on his feet since he landed on his back earlier in the day. She wrapped her fingers delicately around the crux of his elbow and placed her left hand along his shoulder blade. He took his left hand to the top of the doorframe and lifted himself out, not struggling or protesting. Taking in this carnage had drained him of his last bits of fight. Boots took the few steps back that enabled them to move easily past her. As Izzy reached back to shut the door, Boots steadily walked backward, leading the way to the porch. She stealthily watched every bit of Logan's movements with big, steady eyes and furrowed brows. Izzy sucked in the night air and thought that Boots must've been through a lot today, too.

Entering the home, Izzy expected the typical disarray of a bachelor pad. She knew it had once been his family's home, but he'd lived there for several years on his own from her understanding. How would a single guy keep a place like that up? It was big, and he had the ranch to take care of. On the porch, just outside the door, was a foot brush for scraping all the mud from a day out in the muck with the animals. Her mom had incessantly encouraged her father to use those, but he never had. Logan apparently did. Coupled with the bench inside the door where he tucked shoes, mostly boots, neatly beneath it, she realized his secret. This was how the hardwood floors still looked in decent condition. He leaned towards the bench as soon as they walked in, sitting down. He paused and looked down at his boots. Without him having to move much further, Izzy leaned over and pulled them off for him. Glancing up, she joked. "Do I need to remove my shoes as well?"

"Well, that depends. Have you been running around out in the mud? Chasing after any horses lately?"

"Not for a few years, and they're just sandals."

Logan's dimple creased his cheek. "Well, those hospital halls were pretty filthy, but it's up to you."

She sat next to him and casually slipped her shoes off. Removing them made her realize she had no spare clothes, let alone a toothbrush or any other necessities for an overnight stay. They probably should have swung by her house on the way over here. She was so busy making sure he would feel comfortable she hadn't thought about herself.

Logan seemed to read her mind. "I've got spare toothbrushes in the guest bath, and I'm sure one of my T-shirts and pair of gym shorts could work for you to sleep in. Though you'll have to cinch the drawstring up really tight."

Izzy tilted her head a slight bit. "The T-shirt I can picture, a pair of your gym shorts, that will be a sight."

"I normally sleep upstairs, but I'm not sure I should go past the couch tonight. There's a guest room downstairs."

"Maybe I should take the couch. You should have a bed, and I agree that it's best if you stay downstairs. I'm not the best one to be catching you if you get a little woozy going up those stairs tonight."

"I don't know if I can agree with that. If you go around town telling people that's how I treat my female guests, I'll never get a date as long as I live in this town."

"My lips are sealed."

Logan leaned forward, putting his left hand on the edge of the bench. He scratched his forehead lightly with one finger protruding from the cast. "You're a woman who keeps things to herself." He gave her a slight wink and then rocked his body, trying to stand.

She quickly got to her feet and moved to his left side; ready to support him.

His rock forward had been unsuccessful. Logan tilted his head, motioning to the right. She scampered to that side. He lifted his arm and placed his right elbow in her hand, just above the brace they had placed, stretching from his elbow down. It would allow for swelling while they waited a couple of days to place the cast. He seemed to be bothered more by the unfamiliar bulk of it than any pain. She wrapped her other hand just below his armpit and squared her feet. As he stood up, she still wasn't sure where she was taking him. He walked towards the hallway and Boots stayed on their heels.

She vaguely remembered coming to dinner here with her family when she was younger. His dad had been so warm and welcoming, even though she was just the baby sister of the true guests they cared about. The boys had just placed well at some wrestling tournament during their junior year and the dinner was to celebrate. His mom doted on him and had seemed so much more proper than Andres and Izzy's mom.

Logan stopped outside of a door and sheepishly looked over at her.

"What?" She glanced around and down, her irises aglow with her inquisitiveness.

"This is embarrassing."

"Nice, so this might get good. Whatcha need?"

"Well," Logan scratched at his eyebrow, "the nurses help me get dressed before we left the hospital." He paused and Izzy patiently waited. "And I should have thought to make one last pit stop. But really, I haven't been thinking very well this evening."

Izzy tilted her head in a soft laugh. "Is this going where I think it is?"

"Possibly. Yeah." he lifted his left hand to bury his face and gave his head a slight shake. "I can handle most of it, but undoing this belt buckle and unfastening these jeans ain't happening. I don't even know why they put this buckle back on me."

"I saw the twinkle in that nurse's eye when she looked at you. I know exactly why." Izzy gave him a dramatic wink.

Logan threw his head back with a light groan. He couldn't even offer a response.

Izzy continued, "I mean, she's clearly not as interested as Kit, but she definitely showed some interest."

"Enough out of you. Just help me undo my pants and then go get me some sweats."

She gave him a fake glare for being shushed and then moved to open the bathroom door.

"What are you doing?" He asked.

"Taking you into the bathroom?"

"Oh no, I'd feel much better if we just take care of this out here."

"So, I can take your pants off, but I can't be in the bathroom with you." Logan remained deadpan. Izzy threw her hands up. "You're killing me!"

"Give me some little piece of dignity."

"Whatever you need, Logan." Izzy shook her head lightly and leaned into the bathroom to turn on the light so she could even see his belt. She folded in a motion towards kneeling to see how to take it off, but that felt inappropriate. Instead, she tried to keep at least a foot of distance and crane her neck sideways while she tried to make sense of it. Her fingers fumbled as she yanked at all different angles, trying to get it to loosen. Finally, Logan brought his left hand in for assistance.

"Here, let me help you. You pull it here." Logan tugged at the side, the right side, from her vantage point. She realized she just needed to push the rest of the leather down to free it from the catch. She released a satisfactory noise when it popped off and immediately felt the heat rising to her neck.

"Sorry. Clearly, there's not a lot of those in LA."

Logan let out a deep belly laugh, the deepest she'd heard all day.

"Don't worry, this isn't something you had to be qualified to do to move back to Rose River. It's probably not something you'll have to do often."

Izzy bit her lip. What if it was something she *wanted* to do? "Are you implying that because I have a son, I won't have a romantic life in Rose River?"

Logan stammered, "I-I didn't mean to imply anything." There were little beads of sweat forming on his forehead. "I just—I just—" He searched for the right words. "I just didn't want you to feel inadequate."

Now it was Izzy's turn to laugh. "Don't worry, I don't measure my adequacies by my ability to unbuckle a belt. Geez." *However,* she realized, *that may have implications.*

Izzy reached her hands down and, in one fell swoop, released the tension from the top button of Logan's jeans—unwittingly releasing all five of the buttons below. With her fingers lingering inches from the fasteners she'd freed, her shoulders curled in, and her face flushed.

Both of Logan's hands rushed to catch his jeans. Which, fortunately, still held firmly to his hips. The brace on his right arm bumped against Izzy's fingers and heat rose to his cheeks as the sensations in his body alerted him to the autonomous reaction he was having to her impulsive movements.

Izzy's fingers lifted to her lips. "I'll get your sweats." She turned on her heel and walked down the hall.

"My room is at the top of the stairs," Logan called after her. He paused briefly and then continued, "Straight ahead. You'll find my sweats in the bottom right drawer of the dresser. My gym shorts should be there, too. The T-shirts are one drawer up on the left."

Izzy walked dazed, as if she was the one suffering the fog of a concussion.

As Logan made his way into the bathroom, he wondered if it wasn't a ridiculous mistake to have sent her up to his bedroom. Had he even made his bed this morning? What else might be in his drawers? He hadn't had a woman here in years.

He placed a clean toothbrush on the counter next to a tube of toothpaste and heard a soft rapping on the door.

"I have your sweats. If you still want them."

Logan eased open the door, just enough for her to slip the pants through. It took him a while to shimmy the jeans off and wrestle the sweats on, but he managed.

When he made his way into the front room, Izzy was sitting on the couch in a faded blue

T-shirt of his with the collar stretched loose and a frayed edge along the pocket. The light flooding in from the foyer illuminated her upper half, and the shadow of the couch obscured which shorts she had chosen.

"I see you found something." Logan lowered himself down on the other side of the couch, a safe distance from her.

Izzy smoothed her hands across the length of the T-shirt. "Yeah, I left my stuff up in your room. I hope that's okay."

"Yeah, great."

Izzy occupied herself with a frayed string on the edge of his shorts she was wearing as he'd entered the room and lowered himself onto the couch. When she looked up, her jaw fell slack at the sight of his bare chest. It made perfect sense. Filth from the fire and the fall covered the shirt he'd been wearing. They'd even covered her seat with a blanket when they loaded him into her car at the clinic for the drive to the hospital.

The overly attentive nurses at the hospital had found time to give him a bit of a sponge bath and dressed most of his wounds and scrapes. So, he was clean, and the brawny tone of his skin was a gift from the sun and not a result of today's traumas. It had seemed strange for them to put the dirty shirt back on to him, but what choice did they have? They couldn't exactly send him home half-naked. Now that he was home and going to bed, it made sense he'd no longer wear it.

His shoulders were square, his biceps a twist of lean mass earned from years of hard work. She could faintly make out the tan line that bisected his arm from those rare days where the work or weather was rough enough, his shirt stayed on.

She had the urge to reach out and trace her fingers from the nape of his neck down the length of his chest. To feel the way it rose; the tautness of his skin. She dared not look at his abs or the place where the elastic band stretched across his hip bone. She could already feel the heat prickling the back of her neck.

Izzy realized he was observing the way her eyes traced what her fingers dared not touch.

She fumbled for the pillow at her side. "I grabbed this from your bed and found a blanket in the hall closet. Figured I'd give you your pillow, and I'd steal one from the guest room to use here on the couch."

"I think I'll be more comfortable on the couch. You should sleep in the guest room."

Izzy angled her head to the side. And contemplated whether she should argue back.

She relented. "It's your house. I'm gonna give you the final say." She realized he'd had little say over today. "Can I at least make up the couch for you?"

"That would be helpful." Logan held his brace up as evidence and rose to his feet, moving out of her way. Izzy made a quick task of spreading out a fitted sheet he didn't even know he had, and laying the blanket on top. She pulled back the blanket far enough he had a place to sit and still swing his legs into place. She sat down on the coffee table and gave him enough space to maneuver into the bed himself, staying close enough she was there in case he needed help.

"So, you know I'm setting an alarm and waking you up every two hours."

"I figured so much. You seem to be a woman of your word."

"Yes, you could definitely say that. Hopefully, I won't annoy you too much."

Logan eased himself onto the couch, stretched his legs out, and put his head down on the pillow. "Having you here is no annoyance at all."

Izzy leaned over and gently stroked his forehead. It was hard to tell if she was inspecting how well his bandage was still wrapped, or if she was craving one last connection with him.

Logan reached his left hand up and gently traced his fingers on her arm. "I don't think I ever told you thank you."

"I'm sure it's not anything you wouldn't do for most residents of Rose River. It's the least I could do for you."

Logan released a breathy laugh, "I think you overestimate me, Izzy Morales. I would say it is something I would do for you and your brother.

Maybe your mom or your son, but your sister Selena, she'd be out of luck."

"Selena? What's wrong with Selena?"

"Nothing's wrong with Selena." Logan lowered his eyes, looking for words as his fingers continued to trace her arm. Izzy realized her fingers had frozen in place, absorbing his touch.

"Did you know I had a bit of a crush on you in High School?" Logan's eyes bored into hers as he said the words.

Izzy's mouth went slack.

"I did. Don't get me wrong, you were *way* too young for me-"

Izzy cut Logan off before he went further, "The only time we were in school together I was a freshman, and you were a senior and homecoming queen Kit Carlson had her claws so deep into you; no one else existed."

"Aw, I guess that is right. Maybe that was another good reason not to tell you." Logan was holding her arm now, and somehow it rested against his bare chest. Izzy could feel his heartbeat and wanted to spread her fingers out and take in every inch of him.

The cry of a cuckoo clock shattered the moment.

"Ugh, it's midnight. You probably need some sleep." Izzy drew her hand away and savored the slightest bit of resistance that Logan offered.

He's heavily medicated, and he's your big brother's best friend—go to bed!

Izzy slowly pulled herself away and resisted the urge to kiss his cheek after she brought the blanket up over his chest. She wasn't sure the urge was to merely kiss his cheek.

Izzy only took a moment to settle into the guest room. She plugged her phone in with the charger from her purse, set the alarm for two o'clock, and snuggled down into the sheets. She quickly drifted off with the tingle of Logan's fingers still palpable on her arm.

Chapter Eight

When the alarm went off at eight o'clock, Izzy groaned and buried her head deeper in the pillow. Getting up at each of the intervals during the night wasn't bad, but this time she needed to call into work and *stay up*.

All the previous alarms simply meant she had to roll out of the bed and pad down the hall past the nightlight to check on Logan. The ample windows in the front room and lack of curtains meant the moon glow flooded the room, and it never took her eyes long to adjust. She would watch him just for a moment, track the rise and fall of his chest. Each time Boots, dutifully stationed at his feet, looked at her expectantly as though when she woke Logan; everything would be right with the world.

She would touch his arm and say his name softly until his eyes flitted open and, without fail, a smile would spread across his lips. She wondered if it wasn't the lasting effects of the painkillers, especially since he had a fresh dose at 4:00 a.m., but that didn't stop her from basking in its warmth. She noticed how soft she kept her voice, the flirty tone, as if she were ten years younger and discovering a man for the first time.

At this daylight hour, the front room flooded with light as the sun was at full salute. It illuminated the room at the 6 a.m. wake up, but the mountain had helped to shield the house some. She was nervous about what this amount of light may do for him and before she left the guestroom took a moment to draw the curtains and freshen the bed. It would make the most sense to move him in here once she woke him.

"Hey, sleepyhead." Izzy used her body to block the sunlight and positioned her hand as a makeshift visor while Boots had risen to the occasion and was practically standing over him to shade him further. Logan shifted imperceptibly but didn't seem to stir. Izzy ran the back of her hand down the length of his left arm, which was sticking out of the sheets and accessible to her.

"Oh, hey," Logan opened his eyes with the words and immediately twisted his head away from the light, "Oh, wow. It's bright in here."

"It sure is. I was thinking we should move you into the guest room. I already drew the curtains. It's a lot darker in there."

Logan's hand was still over his eyes, but his smile was prominently showing beneath it. "You think of everything."

"I'm a mom. We are programmed that way." She pulled down the blanket and Boots jumped out of the way. "Now come on. We'll play our twenty questions on the way."

Izzy went through all the questions that had become their routine over the last eight hours. What day was it, what his name was, what year was it? He frequently came up with the wrong answers just to taunt her, but they were so clever (and quickly corrected) that she knew he was fine. She set him up in the guest room and wandered back to the kitchen. There was much to do; call into the office, skip work a little longer, and make those pancakes.

Betsy answered the phone at the office. Izzy didn't even bother to ask why it wasn't Fred. Betsy was very understanding, and excited to give everyone an update about how Logan was doing. Izzy grabbed her computer out of the car, so she could have it set up on the counter in case something urgent came up, and went searching for the ingredients to make pancakes. She'd just gotten the batter mixed, and the griddle heated when there was a commotion at the front door. Boots went to the door but wasn't barking, so she figured it was Nate or somebody that was supposed to be there. She looked down at the raggedy T-shirt and shorts and quickly realized she should have prioritized putting on yesterday's clothes over getting breakfast ready. She smoothed her hair and wrapped it into a bun before heading to the entryway.

"Oh, hey Jake!" Izzy self-consciously crossed her arms over her chest and tried to smile as she awkwardly cocked her head to the side. She wasn't sure where Jake lived, but she hadn't seen Logan's brother since she moved back to Rose River. She was a little mad at herself for not even thinking to ask about him during her time at the hospital. She knew Andres had called Logan's mom in Portland, but she wasn't close enough to Logan to know details. She was essentially Andres' substitute cab driver. Surely, Andres informed Jake, right?

Andres just didn't bother to circle back to her.

"Oh, hi." Jake stood up fully and Boots dropped her paws to the floor.

Izzy fell in love with Boots a little more when she walked over and sidled up to Izzy's side—showing she did, in fact, belong. "Are you a friend of Logan's?"

A flash of heat bloomed Izzy's face crimson. "Um, I'm Andres' sister. I'm the one that took Logan to the hospital in Junction City and they asked me to stay with him last night. Aren't you his brother?"

"Oh, right." Jake's head nodded in agreement, but his eyes did not register who she was or why she was there. Still.

"Logan is just in the guest room, resting. I was just making something for breakfast while I checked my work e-mail."

Jake wandered into the living room as if to inspect. And make sure everything was where it should be. He noted the blanket and pillow on the couch, which she was grateful for. She wasn't about to explain that she'd slept in the guest room. It would complicate things too much at the moment. The silence was killing her.

"I woke him up every two hours, just as they asked me to. I asked him the questions to make sure he was okay. The last time was at 8, so I won't need to wake him again until

10. Although I might get him up sooner for breakfast."

Jake didn't respond. He continued to walk around the front room and then circled towards the hall, "I'll just go check on him, make sure he's okay."

Izzy buried her head in both of her hands. She must look like a crazy person—taking over the kitchen, wearing Logan's clothes. Meanwhile, poor Logan was in the other room asleep, recovering from a concussion; after he'd lost most of his ranch and a wildfire had threatened his house.

She shook her head, gave a quick pat of gratitude to Boots, and turned back to the kitchen to turn off the griddle. *Where did Jake even live? Why hadn't he ridden in on his high horse last night? He could've taken him to the hospital.*

She headed upstairs to put on yesterday's clothes. It would probably be a better move in this situation than finishing the pancakes. When she came back downstairs. Jake was sitting at the table in the kitchen with his phone in his hand.

"Oh, hey, I just talked to my mom. Apparently, Andres explained to her you would be here. But she hadn't thought to explain that to me, otherwise, I probably wouldn't have rushed here. Sorry if I was brusque earlier." He sat the phone down and clasped his hands.

"I'm sure it looked a little strange."

"Someone cooking in this kitchen? Most definitely." Jake's face had softened a little. "To be honest, I wasn't even sure the forest fire was legitimate. I saw something on the news, but it didn't sound like it was anywhere near the town or close to here. It mostly seemed like mom was making a ploy to get me over here for the weekend. She'll be here too, in a few hours."

"Oh, that makes sense." Izzy shifted her weight from one leg to the other. "I should get out of your way. I'm glad he'll have family here." Izzy moved quickly to her computer, gathering her things.

"I would love pancakes, and if you have the time, I would love to hear a little more first-hand what happened. Currently, all I have is what I heard from my mother, which she heard through your brother. And I don't think my brothers up to sharing anything right now."

"Let the poor lady leave if she wants to."

Izzy spun around at the sound of Logan's voice. "What are you doing out of bed? You should be resting."

"I've been resting enough. Besides, someone needs to catch my brother up on all the goings on around here." Logan leaned with his left hand against the counter to brace himself. Jake didn't move from the table.

"You look even worse standing up, brother." Jake shook his head in judgment.

"Here, let me help you." Izzy took half a step towards Logan when the tilt of Logan's head and harshness in his eyes shut her down. This wasn't what he wanted right now, even if it was what he needed.

Izzy's discomfort was registering off the scales. Somehow Logan made it to the table, Jake offered to finish pancakes, and she managed to exit.

No hug, no last touch, no final words, just awkward.

Chapter Nine

T he rain was a welcome sight as Izzy rounded the corner to pull into her mom's. It was barely a drizzle, but the layers of dark gray in the distance clarified that it would soon let loose. Ordinarily, she would complain about rain in late August, but after the parched July and record heat, with wildfires creeping to the coastal mountain range, it was appreciated. The bit of moisture from the night before and the promised rain tonight would be a welcome buffer to keep the fire at bay and help with its containment. Besides, this was the Oregon Coast. Summer rain was a given.

It also helped to justify the fact she was in yoga pants and her favorite sweatshirt. After her strange morning, she opted to work from home and took a quick shower during her lunch break, throwing on whatever felt most comfortable. She was still groggy from the lack of sleep and the strange happenings of the night before. As she reached for her car door, the Imperial Death March called out from her purse. Her cheeks perked up, with a smile creasing her lips. Her ex, Victor, had worked in sound effects in Hollywood *and* been a Star Wars fanatic. Making this his ring tone had been a minor form of revenge, but it brought her tiny moments of joy. Her son liked the deep punctuated cadence and had a march that went with it. He did not know the connotations that accompanied it as well. The ring had run its course and gone to voicemail before she reached the door.

Marco wrapped himself around her as though it had been a year since he had seen her. The warmth of his pudgy arms always seemed to make the rest of the world a little more bearable. Everything was tolerable when this little guy was her reward.

"Mama, the baby chicks aren't babies no more!" he said, pulling her towards the back door. She tossed her purse on the counter and gave her mom a quick peck on the cheek as Marco dragged her to the back patio. She thought about rain boots and coats and determined that making it quick was a better plan. Her mom was making dinner and if they didn't escape soon, they would be there all night and she just wanted the comforts of home.

Marco had corralled one of the fledgling chicks and was getting in the bit of petting she promised him, when her mom was calling to her from the patio. Elena was waving something in the air. Izzy gave a glance to assure Marco was content and made her way to her mom.

"What is it?"

"Phone call." Elena held Izzy's phone up like a prize.

Izzy's eyes narrowed and her lips tightened. "Why are you answering my phone?"

"Why are you leaving it in my kitchen?" Her mom's eyebrows conveyed she would always have the upper hand. "I've got Marco." Elena held the phone inside the door for her. "You go on inside."

Izzy released an exasperated breath and relented.

"Hello?"

"Oh, hey Iz."

Izzy's feet locked in place. Only one person called her Iz and she evaded his phone call not ten minutes ago.

"What do you want, Vic?"

"Well, great to hear your voice, too." Victor's words hung in the air and Izzy negotiated with her body to function normally. Her heart rate wouldn't cooperate, but she managed to close the sliding glass door and walk to the kitchen to sit on a stool. She didn't have any words for him, though. She wasn't the one who made the call.

"So, anyway," Victor said, "I just wanted to confirm for next Saturday and that I'll have Marco for a week."

"What do you mean you'll have Marco for a week?"

"Well, our agreement stipulates that I can have him for 3 weeks every summer, so the least I should get is the last week of summer."

Izzy tilted her head back and closed her eyes. *Just breathe.* "You honestly think you can call with one week's notice and take your son for a week?"

"I can. If I require you to meet me halfway, I need to give you a month's notice. If not, I don't. I've rented a place in Ashland, so he and I will just be in Oregon for the week."

Izzy tried to remember the details of their agreement. She remembered that taking Marco out of California was a lot harder than she imagined it would be, and there were a lot of concessions. The lawyers did most of the negotiating and she mostly shrugged things off.

She just needed away from Vic and to be near people who would help her raise her son.

Her chest heaved as she released the breath she didn't realize she'd been holding. "Fine, what time? We'll meet at my mom's house."

"I'm sure Marco wants to show me his room and all of his things. I'll just pick him up at your house."

"Not this time, Vic. Not with this little notice. What time?" Her heartbeat rang in her ears as it intensified.

"Whatever. Four o'clock, but don't be late. He and I will still have a drive ahead of us."

"We aren't the ones who have trouble with reading a clock, Vic. Just don't forget to feed him dinner."

"You are always so bitter, Iz. This is why I never wanted to be around you."

"Hanging up now." Izzy put the phone down to the counter so fast she almost forgot to disconnect the call. Once she realized it, she started rapidly pressing the screen as though she were playing whack-a-mole, making sure he was gone.

"Everything alright sweetie?" Elena's voice sent a shock through Izzy's spine, and she jolted to sit straight.

"Yeah, mom. All's good." She looked down at Marco. "Guess what, little man? You get to go on an adventure with your dad—he's coming to get you a week from tomorrow!"

Marco's eyes lit up and grew the size of saucers, and he sprang his body as though he were on a coil.

Izzy bit her lip and wondered if she should've waited to tell him until she knew for sure, or until Victor was here- let it be a surprise. She released her breath and tried to remind herself that Vic usually showed up for Marco. He was just late. He was slow to prioritize, but he usually came through.

"Come on, help me set the table." Elena led her grandson to the kitchen and Izzy realized they were stuck for the evening. At least she didn't have to cook.

Her mom squeezed her arm as she walked back towards the dining room. "Aren't you glad you're single, dear? Don't need men like that messing up your life."

Izzy gave a slow nod and closed her eyes.

A ding from her phone brought her attention back.

It was a text from Logan:

> THANKS AGAIN FOR
> EVERYTHING. I NEED
> TO FIND A WAY TO
> MAKE IT UP TO YOU.

Chapter Ten

Logan heard the crunch of the tires as his mom pulled up. His eyes lingered on the scorched remains of what had been his livelihood and his joy. His fingers ran the worn edges of his straw cowboy hat. He lifted it to his nose and breathed in the musky grit of smoke and ash; it was miraculous it survived the carnage. He imagined it may never smell the same again.

"Why, hello son," Belle's voice was overly bright. "You'll never guess who I saw on my way up here."

Logan turned slowly towards her, weighing the pros and cons of playing along with the everything-is-fine fantasy versus trying to have a real conversation about all the destruction and what needed to be done. Most folks would've been itching for their mom to arrive in a crisis like this. He would've been just fine with her offering her opinion over the phone and him having the choice of when he would answer.

He offered a shrug and busied himself with dusting off his hat.

"Why, Kit! Did you know she is working as a nurse at the clinic now? She looked just lovely. She was walking by the Garden Spot when I stopped in to give Mrs. Beasley my best and pick up some lunch for all of us. She was dressed in these cute lavender scrubs and everything."

Logan ran his tongue along his teeth. "I think Andres mentioned she was a medical assistant there."

"Nurse, assistant, it's all the same thing. Point is that she is doing good things for herself while she is waiting to settle down with the right guy and become a mother."

Logan shielded the sun with his hat for a second before deciding he might as well put it on. "Thanks for bringing lunch. Let me help you get your things."

"Don't avoid the topic, Logan. You aren't getting younger, and she is the most eligible gal in this town. You two looked so lovely as Homecoming King and Queen. It surprised me you didn't get married straight out of high school."

Logan walked straight to her Escalade and started getting things out of the back with his one good arm. He was hoping she had two bags because she overpacked and not because she planned to stay long.

"Actually, sweetie, all of this could be a wonderful opportunity for you. Sell what's left of this mess, head back to school, and finish your engineering degree. You could even stay with me and go to school in Portland!" Belle's words rushed out of her mouth and heightened in pitch.

Logan couldn't help but roll his eyes. He shut the back gate, hoisted one bag up onto his right shoulder, delicately moving it past the brace, and grabbed the other bag with his good arm. The screen door squeaked as Jake came out to the porch.

"Hello, mom."

"Oh, Jake, so glad you're here already." She looked back at Logan. "Or law school! You could become a lawyer, just like Jake. Wouldn't that be lovely? The two of you could practice together."

Jake patted Logan's shoulder sympathetically as Logan walked past, but he knew better than to speak up. "Oh, here, let me grab the door for you." Jake moved past him and pulled open the screen.

"Yep, wouldn't make any sense for you to grab the bags or anything." Mentally Logan finished the comment, *'after all, you're the lawyer and I'm just the ranch hand who never finished college.'*

"Actually, Jake, be a dear and grab the food off the passenger seat before it gets too warm in the sun. I have sandwiches, fruit salad, and veggies from the Garden Spot."

"Sure." Jake bounded down the steps and Belle followed Logan into the house.

"Guess what else I saw on the way up?"

Logan was scared to ask. He was sure he didn't want the answer. Didn't matter though, turns out the question was rhetorical.

"A news van! They were positioned near the base of the road with a view of the mountain behind them- it was a great shot with the smoke and everything. Turns out they had no idea half of our property burned down. Of course, I didn't know the full of it, but Tony and Nate had filled me in a little, so the news crew interviewed me! I think they want to interview you too. They had no idea you were injured." Belle shook her head and put her hand to her heart.

Logan inhaled deeply, but his haunches were up and there was electricity crackling in his veins.

"Mom, this is nobody's business but ours. This doesn't need to be on the news. I don't even know what's going on yet. I haven't even talked to Tony and Nate- I am barely up and walking around- I don't even have my cast on yet. Can you let me catch my breath?"

Belle pushed her weight back on her heels. It looked like she may fall over. Her children didn't speak to her like this. "Logan Matthew Roberts- you are *not* the only person this happened to. You need to check yourself."

The screen door pulled back on its springs, closing with a creak and a smash announcing Jake had joined them.

"I'm taking a shower." Logan set his mom's bags on the couch and headed to his room upstairs, totally unsure of how to do this with his arm in a brace.

Chapter Eleven

"Are you wearing that blue just to torment me? You know how good I think it looks on you."

Izzy rolled her eyes, but she couldn't help the way her lips curled up over the compliment. Dr. Carrington took that as a success and winked with his wave as he continued past her door.

Friday morning was a little more relaxed at the clinic. They tried to keep a lighter schedule for last-minute appointments before the weekend. After working from home the day before, Izzy was keeping her door open, making it clear she was accessible if anyone needed her. Betsy had already stopped in with checks to sign and Raya had checked in about Logan. Izzy stumbled a minute before she realized no one needed to know she had stayed at his house. They were only asking because she was the one that took him to the hospital. His condition leaving the hospital, vague details was all she needed to share.

Izzy had started three texts to Logan the night before when she'd gotten home after dinner at her mom's. She hadn't sent any of them. She didn't know what to say and all the words felt off. She also knew his family was there and the interaction with his brother had put her off a bit. She vaguely remembered his mom. From her memory, Belle Roberts had always seemed like someone who liked things the way she liked them; and definitely how she planned them.

Besides, there wasn't anything to be said after his brief thank you- he hadn't exactly left an open door. So, it had surprised her when she got a second note from him when she was climbing into bed.

> HAVE YOU THOUGHT OF A WAY I CAN MAKE IT UP TO YOU?

It had made her giggle like she did when she caught a boy's eye when she was fifteen. She wrote her response and deleted it many times, glad that Marco was already in bed so that she wasn't ignoring him.

> HOW ABOUT WE FIGURE THAT OUT ONCE YOU'VE HEALED?

His response came quickly-

> BUT THEN I DON'T HAVE AN EXCUSE

TO SEE YOU THIS
WEEKEND.

She had a satisfactory grin on her face and a little heat in her cheeks when she went to respond. The morning had ended so abruptly she was sure she had imagined pieces of last night. This time she was more pointed-

WHAT ABOUT YOUR
FAMILY — AREN'T
THEY STILL IN
TOWN?

He quickly fired back-

WHY? YOU WANT
TO SEE THEM TOO?

His response elicited a howl of laughter from Izzy that had her clutching her mouth for fear of waking her son.

NOT REALLY, BUT I AM SURE THEY ARE HOPING TO SPEND TIME WITH YOU.

MY MOM HAS PLANS WITH FRIENDS TOMORROW NIGHT AND JAKE WENT BACK TO EUGENE TONIGHT. HE'S WRAPPING SOME THINGS UP AT HIS OFFICE TOMORROW AND COMING BACK ON SUNDAY. HE THINKS HE'LL BE HERE A FEW DAYS HELPING TO SORT THINGS OUT WITH THE INSURANCE COMPANY AND SUCH.

As she read his words, Izzy twiddled her hair between her fingers. She was contemplating leaving Marco with her mom again. But it felt so soon after him staying there the night before; especially knowing that the following weekend she would lose him for a week. She'd never been without him for more than a night before.

In the end, she hadn't promised Logan anything. She said she would try to bring him dinner, and Marco might be with her.

This morning, she hadn't quite worked up the courage to text her mom about taking Marco. What would she tell her? She found her mind constantly wandering with the idea of it, though...

"Oh, Andres!" Izzy leaped to her feet when she glimpsed him walking past her door. "I've been meaning to chat with you."

Andres took a step in reverse and turned into her office. "And I've been meaning to talk to you." His head tilted slightly and his tone clearly showed he was unhappy about something.

"Okay," Izzy shrugged slightly, "you first."

"I understand that most of my life you have known me as Andres, but in these walls, *especially*, I am Dr. Morales. As the director at this clinic, I think you should understand and respect that."

Izzy's shoulders went limp. He was completely right. She needed to do better at that. She stammered slightly. She wanted to make excuses. However, she knew this wasn't the first or only time. "I... I truly am sorry." She searched deeper. "You are absolutely accurate in calling me on this, and I need to do better. I will work on it and..." She tried to think of some way to make it up to him but came up short. "Please let me know if you catch me doing it again. Correct me in public if you need to. I'll deserve it and respond appropriately."

Andres' posture softened slightly. He had braced himself unnecessarily for a fight. "I'll remind you in private after. I am sure it is a bit of adjustment. Maybe I should start calling you Ms. Morales. Would that help?"

"No! Please don't. If people hear me called that and they don't know our family—they'll think I'm your wife. Better to call me Isabella. I should work on that with everyone at some point. Izzy is lax for the Director."

"I'll work on it," he nodded with a grave look in his eyes. He was giving this way more importance than Izzy felt it warranted. Most likely a reflection of how important it was for him. He continued, "What did you need?"

"Oh, mine is a personal favor. Should I ask you outside of work?" Izzy scrunched her nose up and raised her eyebrows slightly.

"If it's quick, go ahead."

"Well, Victor is coming up this weekend to get Marco," the words tumbled out in one exhale. "He's getting him from mom's, and it would be nice to have you there... to..." *to what?* She wasn't sure herself. To punch Vic if he was a jerk? To hold her back so she wasn't a jerk in front of her kid? To intimidate Vic?

Andres reached out his hand and firmly squeezed Izzy's forearm, "I got you. You don't need to explain this."

The heat that pricked the back of her eyes and the lump in her throat surprised her. She'd been doing it on her own for so long that she forgot what it felt like to have support.

Kit poked her head in the office, breaking the moment. "Did you have fun playing nurse to Logan yesterday?"

Andres spun to her before Izzy could even react. "Logan is essentially our brother, Kit. Izzy took him to the hospital because I couldn't get away from the clinic. She would never date her brother and stop making implications otherwise. Don't you have work to do?"

Kit pulled her chin back and widened her eyes. Izzy wasn't sure if this was the first time Andres had witnessed one of Kit's incessant little attacks on her, or if this one was the proverbial straw, but it had certainly taken Kit by surprise.

Kit raised her hand to her heart. "I wasn't implying anything. I was only asking after Logan. He's a friend to all of us."

Andres' audible exhale made it clear he wasn't buying it, but he stretched his hand towards Izzy so she could respond directly.

"Um, I don't know how he is. I left as soon as his family got there. He was stable, and all bandaged up when we left the hospital. He'll need a cast put on his distal forearm fracture once the swelling goes down, but mostly he just needs to rest. Shouldn't be anything that time won't heal." Izzy was self-conscious as she summarized for two people that worked in medical. It's probably why her brain conjured distal forearm fracture over simply saying his broken wrist.

"Oh, glad to hear." Kit pulled herself up to her full six feet in height and walked on down the hall.

"I'm sure you need to get back to work," Andres turned to the door, "Oh, but hey," he paused before turning back, "don't worry about checking in on Logan anymore. I shouldn't have burdened you with it, especially when you have Marco. You've done more than enough."

"Oh, well, Marco had drawn him a picture I thought I might drop by with some enchiladas or something tonight."

"Don't bother. I'll just bring him some pizza and beer. Take your weekend. I am sure he'll need enchiladas and pictures next week after his mom has left town." With that, Andres turned and left her office.

Izzy couldn't help but wonder if there was something Andres knew she didn't.

Chapter Twelve

Belle Roberts didn't seem to understand the workings of a concussion, either that or she didn't much care. She had fired so much at Logan over the 30 hours since she pulled into town that he would need a dark room and a compress even if he hadn't had his head slammed against the dirt floor of a barn packed so hard it may well have been concrete. She'd left at 5:00 p.m. for some social obligation and he'd been lying still on the couch with cool pressure on his eyes and a soft cushion under his head ever since. Boots was diligently resting her head on his belly so that giving her pets took no effort at all.

He wasn't asleep, but in that place where the mind drifts. Questions about the property, the insurance, the animals flooded him; everything. He was grateful that Tony and Nate, with the help of the guys from George's ranch down the road, had spent hours after taking him to the clinic searching for all the animals. There had been 5 or 6 unaccounted for—2 horses, and a few cows, but each one of those had wandered back on their own, with Daisy being the last one to show up earlier that day. If she'd been smart enough to leave with the other horses, she might've been found with them too. He didn't dwell on that, though. She was okay. George was boarding them all for the moment and the big question was what to do about it all. Hurry and rebuild, hoping George's hospitality would last? Sell most all of 'em and start anew once things settled into place next spring or a year from now?

His mother had wild ideas about selling the whole thing. The insurance company dragging their feet on the wildfire qualifying did not help this, along with their uncertainty about how much the outbuildings were even worth. So, most everything was speculative.

Every once in a while, thoughts of Izzy would cut through the haze. The way she twisted her raven hair deftly into a bun and yet strands simply fell in little cascades that made it look messy and carefree. The gentle touch of her fingertips. The depth and warmth of her sandy-colored eyes.

The doorbell pulled Logan from his thoughts. Boots heard it too and panted expectantly. Logan patted her head. "With any luck, that'll be Izzy with our dinner." Izzy had made no promises or even gotten back to him about coming over, but there wasn't anyone else he was expecting.

He smoothed his hair as he passed the mirror in the hall, grateful he had gotten his wound covered with a smaller bandage. At least he looked a little less like a mummy unevenly wrapped in layers. He ran his hands over his shirt, but there wasn't much to do about the wrinkles. He tried to contain his grin, but in the end, it only made it look lopsided.

He sucked in a deep breath and slowly pulled open the door.

"Andres." Logan stumbled back half a step.

"You look surprised to see me." Andres gave him a sideways glance and then squeezed past him into the house. "You should know I do house calls for you. How's my patient? I brought you pizza."

Logan felt his heart racing slightly. What if Izzy came by and her brother was there? He hadn't even thought that through. As if reading his mind, Andres continued his monologue. "I ran into Izzy earlier. She was being sweet and mentioned she might bring food by for you. I told her not to worry. Her shift was up. She'd done enough. It was my turn to step up and take care of things. After all, you need professional medical care, and I am qualified.

"So I told her I'd bring over dinner and check in on things. Besides, I think people at the clinic were thinking something might be going on between you guys and I couldn't do that to her."

Andres didn't even look up as his words cut into Logan like little spears—*do that to her?*

"Where's your mom at? I even got a smaller Hawaiian pizza for her, so we didn't have to hear guff about our menagerie of meats!"

Logan sucked in air through his teeth and slowly shut the door. It would take a minute to take in everything. It was as though Izzy was the only person who understood you had to move a little quieter and slower for someone who just got a concussion.

"Moms out for the night, but I'm sure she'll appreciate your thought when she gets back home." Logan dismissed the rest of it and walked into the kitchen, where Andres was already pulling down plates and serving up pizza for them both. "I had been meaning to send you a note. I need a cast on my arm, but they wanted the swelling to go down first. I can go back to Junction City for it, but it sounded like it was something you could do?"

"Oh yeah, let me look at that. We should probably do that tomorrow if it's ready. You can just meet me down at the clinic. No charge. Just don't tell Dr. Carrington. He doesn't seem to understand how we do things around here." Logan sat down and rested his arm on the table. Andres pulled back the wrap and gently moved things around to look under the brace.

"It's looking pretty good. It should be ready for the cast by tomorrow. So, no need for a pin, 'eh? Wasn't sure from the X-rays we took. That fall you took was pretty hard." Andres wrapped the arm back up and washed his hands before bringing over the pizza and some paper towels. "I was going to grab us beer but figured that wasn't the best mix with your concussion and medications."

The men spent a few moments in silence. Logan picked the meats off the top of his pizza and Andres steadily ate his without lowering the slice back to the plate; as if he hadn't taken a minute to eat all day. Once he finished his first slice, he paused a moment.

"Do you want to talk about it?" Andres' hands rested on the edge of the table, and he looked at Logan with genuine concern. It dawned on Logan that all this talking wasn't in Andres' nature. He wasn't sure how to handle this messed up situation either. At least there was some honesty in that.

Logan gave a slight shake of his head.

Andres nodded in return, and they sat in silence.

Logan's belly grumbled, and he started eating the pizza rather than just picking at it. The silence made it easier to breathe and to eat.

"Have you met Willa?" Andres' question punctuated the quiet they'd settled into. Andres had finished four slices of pizza and Logan was steadily working on his second.

"Don't think so."

"She's new to town. Social worker at the clinic."

"Oh, wait—I saw her. She was the only person I didn't recognize in the uproar when I first woke up. Long light brown hair?" Logan squinted slightly, trying to bring her into focus.

"Yeah, that's her," Andres said and then fiddled with his napkin.

"Is there a reason you bring that up?" Logan knew Andres well enough to know there was a reason, and well enough to know if Logan inferred a reason, Andres would shut down.

"Nah, not really. I just enjoy spending time with her. Only at work, obviously. We take walks sometimes. She's a nice girl."

Logan nodded his head and tried to hide his smirk. Andres never brought girls up. This must mean something.

Andres let out a steady breath and then looked up expectantly. "Oh, what about you and Kit? That girl is still stuck on you."

Logan's eyes rolled towards the ceiling. "Not you, too."

"What does that mean?"

"It means everyone seems to have forgotten that she and I have a history and that I have *no interest* in her," Logan's head dropped back. "She's only interested in me because she's gone through every other guy in this town."

"I've never dated her." Andres' voice was hard to read. Logan wasn't sure if this bothered him, or he was trying to prove a point.

"Well, you are welcome to," Logan replied.

"No chance of that." Andres shook his head slightly for emphasis as he pushed back his chair and grabbed both their plates.

"And yet you think I should date her?"

"I don't know if I would go that far. Just letting you know that you have options. That's one thing this town seems to be short on." Andres rinsed the plates and set them in the dishwasher.

Logan rubbed the back of his neck with his good hand. There was only one option in this town he had an interest in, and he was pretty sure that Andres wouldn't be okay with that.

Chapter Thirteen

"**T**hanks for being here, Andres." Izzy squeezed his hand. Marco finished hugging him and ran straight into the kitchen for some of Grandma Elena's pozole.

Andres squeezed her hand back and shook her arm slightly. "Is Victor going to be pissed that you fed Marco immediately before he picked him up?"

"Do you think I care what Victor thinks?" Izzy's eyebrows shot up. "I much prefer him to have two dinners than none. Besides, it's only 3:30. This is practically a snack."

"I'm on your side, remember?" Andres pulled Izzy into his side.

Izzy inhaled deeply and let it out slowly. "I may need to do a little more deep breathing before he arrives."

"Might not be a bad idea." Andres ruffled her hair slightly.

Victor's arrival went smoother than she had expected. Perhaps it was the extra support of family that made it easier. Or maybe their presence had Victor on his best behavior. It really didn't matter. What mattered was that the first time Marco had seen his parents together since they had moved to Oregon, they were civil to each other; almost cordial. Marco was finally the focus, as he always should've been.

Sitting at the table with her mother and brother, they took the opportunity to reminisce and laugh a little. They even called their sister Selena, who was camping for the weekend, and made her jealous she couldn't come to join them.

"Mija, I'm so glad you are finally home." Elena smoothed Izzy's hair and pulled her close, stopping her from clearing the table. "It was hard having you so far away."

"I missed you too, mom," Izzy buried her head in her mom's shoulder and thought of a million nights in LA when she had wished for exactly this.

A kitchen towel lightly hit Izzy's shoulder and fell on the floor next to her.

"Hey, what was that?" Elena swatted her hand towards Andres.

"You guys were getting too serious. Let's clean this up- I have a documentary waiting at home."

Izzy wagged her head. "You are the most boring person on the planet."

"You mean smartest, I think you mean smartest." Andres strained his neck towards Izzy, slightly shaking his head—as though resisting the urge to stick his tongue out at her.

"Enough you two! You are reminding me how joyous it is to live alone! Here, Izzy, I am going to package up some of this soup. Why don't you bring it over to Logan? I'm sure he could use a meal on standby with all he has to sort out." Elena carried the pot to the kitchen.

"I can take it over there, mom. No need for Izzy to do it." Andres said.

Elena called back over her shoulder, "But what about your precious documentary?"

Andres mouthed the words 'precious documentary' in a clear act of protest.

"It's no big deal Andres. The ranch isn't too far out of my way, and unlike you and mom, I am not skilled in how to use my alone time just yet."

Andres shrugged. "If you don't mind. While you are there, try talking him into going back to school."

Izzy's head snapped back as if someone had slapped her. "I should what?"

"Oh, his mom is on this kick that they should sell the ranch and he should finish his engineering degree. I think she feels guilty he gave up school to run the ranch when his dad died. This seems a good time to get out. He has it financially solvent and with the insurance money, they might even get a little more out of it if they sell it now." Andres pulled grapes off his mom's sideboard and popped them in his mouth as he casually spoke.

Izzy's jaw was slack. "Is that what he wants?"

"Of course not. Or at least not yet. He's sentimental. He's attached to that property. He doesn't realize he can't run a ranch forever and we aren't getting younger. He needs his degree."

"He doesn't *need* a degree—that's just your opinion. He's got along just fine for years without one." Izzy could feel the hairs on the back of her neck standing up.

"Look, I've got a doctorate, you've got a master's degree—we shouldn't deny him that same opportunity." Andres shrugged, as though his point was obvious.

"We? We shouldn't deny him? We aren't denying him anything. I'm just saying it's his choice. Of course, he should go back to school if *he* wants—but not if that's what you want, or his mom wants. Being a fulfilled, happy person is way more important than having a degree.

He should do what he wants, what he loves." It surprised Izzy how swiftly the words poured out of her.

"Just because you think he belongs in this small town doesn't mean he has to stay here." Andres threw his comment off the cuff. "You wouldn't even give a guy the time of day unless he had a degree similar or better than yours."

"Are you serious?" Izzy's eyebrows launched to their fullest height. "I dated plenty of guys with degrees, and where did that get me? You know very well Vic was getting his master's degree when Marco was little. Look where holding out for that got me. Just because a guy makes good money or has an impressive degree does not make him a good person. What the hell did they do to you in medical school to make you so high on yourself and judgmental of everyone else?"

"He's my best friend Izzy. I think I know him pretty well. Don't worry about saying anything. I doubt he'd listen to you, anyway." Andres shrugged his shoulders and shook his head slightly. "Hey mom, I'm taking this peach.

Love you!" Andres grabbed the peach out of the bowl. Elena called her goodbye from the kitchen, and he had little left to say to Izzy. "See you at work on my Monday, kiddo."

Izzy's veins were still pumping when Andres walked out the front door. Maybe she was getting worked up over nothing, or maybe Logan was stuck in a world where no one really saw him.

Chapter Fourteen

Logan looked at his phone again. He hadn't heard from Izzy all week, and honestly thought he'd offended her. He figured sending Andres over with dinner instead of coming herself was a pretty clear signal.

There it was in black and white, though:

IF YOU'RE AROUND

I HAVE SOME OF

MY MOM'S POZOLE I

CAN DROP BY.

Nothing in the note addressed her silence for the entire week, but it promised she was coming over, and that was all he needed. He responded quickly, not taking time to remember it was in his best interest to play it cool and take his time to write back. After all, it was Saturday night. Did he need to make it obvious he was home alone, doing nothing? Fortunately, she responded quickly as well; she'd be there in less than half an hour.

He rushed to clean the kitchen, not because it was that dirty, but because he had already made himself dinner and he didn't want her to know. His new cast made it easier to get around. It felt as though it reinforced his arm, and he didn't have to be so careful.

His head wound had stopped weeping, so he no longer needed bandages wrapping the circumference of his head. They had shaved the surrounding area, so earlier in the week, he'd gone to see Clarice at the barbershop. Her hands were shaking the entire time, but she used the clippers to trim up everything else and blend it with the shaved area that led to puckered stitches.

He would still wear ball caps and cowboy hats as much as possible, but he felt less self-conscious when there wasn't a two-inch length difference to highlight his wound. He hadn't had his hair this short since he was in high school, and it felt strange to have to coerce it into place. Clarice had even given him a complimentary container of something she called 'hair clay' to help him with it. He much preferred when his hair was long enough he could just wash it and ignore it.

He heard a light tapping on the door, which was mostly the screen bouncing against the frame. He smiled to himself and made a mental note that Izzy wasn't one for doorbells.

He ducked past the mirror in the hallway, knowing the distraction of his hair would keep him at least another five minutes, and swung open the door. The mid-height blonde with heels, a suit jacket, and a microphone was not who he expected.

"Are you Logan Roberts?"

His eyes volleyed between her and the cameraman behind her, trying to decide if he should answer that.

"Is that thing running?" was all he managed.

"Oh, not yet. We are hoping to interview you live." Her cheeks rose as she flashed him a beguiling smile.

"I'm sorry, ma'am. I'm not interested in being interviewed." Logan stepped back to shut the door.

"No need to call me ma'am," her lips tightened and pulled slightly from the smile. "I'm Serena Johnson from KGAW in Portland. We are doing a piece that we hope will gain national coverage. Folks are interested in what's happening with the wildfires in Oregon right now. You are one of the few ranches it directly impacted. People want to hear your story."

"Not much of a story, I'm afraid. We're just fine." Logan edged the door toward closing when Serena whipped open the screen door and charged forward a step, placing her in the doorframe.

She must've jumped back three feet and nearly twisted her heel when Boots came charging to the door, with two decisive barks and teeth bared as she maintained a steady growl. Logan had a hard time keeping the smirk off his face while he held the screen door open, allowing Boots to serve as the barrier.

Serena adjusted her jacket slightly and smoothed the end of her bobbed flaxen hair. She cleared her throat and continue—speaking louder to compensate for Boots. "Belle Roberts was the one who suggested we speak to you. She's given us permission to take footage of the property." The woman did not know her words were only decreasing her chances. Logan could feel the muscles in his shoulders tensing.

The woman wasn't one for subtle clues, and continued, "Didn't I hear you got injured?" her eyes were on his cast and rendered the question rhetorical. "Weren't you saving one of your animals?"

"I think he was pretty clear with his answer." Izzy hadn't come into sight, but her voice was commanding, and you'd never guess it came from a woman hardly over five feet tall. Boots gave a welcoming bark and trotted in her direction.

Ms. KGAW stepped back and the cameraman also turned.

Izzy tousled the fur on Boots' head and let the dog fall in step beside her. Izzy's sandals hardly made a sound as they padded onto the first wooden step of the porch. She wasn't even making eye contact with the news crew and instead looked steadily at Logan. Her hair was down, cascading past her shoulders and the sun angling down in the west seemed to accentuate the way it wrapped around the curve of her neck. Even eight feet away, Logan had to wrap his fingers into a loose fist to fight the urge to reach out towards her.

She was in jeans and a fitted rose-colored T-shirt. A sexy contrast to her uptight work attire, or even the loose shape of his T-shirt and gym shorts. The color looked amazing on her.

It seemed to brighten her eyes and highlight the flush in her cheeks.

"Pozole." Izzy held up the bag, presenting it with a crooked smile and a tilt of her head. She continued towards him, lacing past the others with Boots at her side as if they didn't even exist.

Ms. KGAW tried again, "Mr. Roberts, we only need a few moments of your time."

"Actually, I'm a little busy at the moment." He nodded towards Izzy and then pushed the screen door fully open so Izzy could easily bypass the reporter.

"We could do this another time. I'm in town all day tomorrow as well."

Logan's eyes didn't leave Izzy.

"I'll leave my card." Ms. KGAW surrendered defeat with a deep exhale.

"You can just set it on the rail." Logan nodded that direction and closed both doors, turning to follow Izzy towards the kitchen.

"I guess it's a good thing the temperature dropped below 65. We all know soup cannot be consumed when it's over 70." He winked as he took the package from her, lightly brushing his fingers against her hand during the exchange.

She bantered back that this soup could be consumed in *any* weather and that prejudices like this meant she shouldn't allow him to eat it. Logan couldn't take his eyes off of her. He didn't even care what she was saying as long as her lips were moving and he could hear the lilt of her voice.

Logan leaned against the counter and watched as she deftly moved about the kitchen. Pulling out pots; finding spoons, cutting boards, and knives. She was heating the soup on the stove rather than throwing it in the microwave and pulling out avocados and cabbage to freshly slice for toppings. He loved the way her hair would fall forward each time she bent to get something. And the way she seemed so comfortable. She never even asked a question of him about where anything might be. She just made herself at home.

Logan inched up behind Izzy when she stood still for a few moments stirring the soup at the stove. He reached out his fingers and ran them through the ends of her hair that fell along her mid-back. Brushing against the soft material of her T-shirt on the other side.

"What are you doing?" Izzy shook her head slightly as though she was flicking away a fly. Logan was undeterred as he slid his left hand from the edge of her shoulder to the curve of her waist and cradled her there. He took his arm awkwardly bound in a cast and swept her hair from her left side across her right shoulder and leaned his lips towards her neck. He gently breathed there just for a moment. His exhale tickled her skin. Izzy closed her eyes and took a sharp inhale, feeling her flesh ripple in response to his touch. He first brushed his lips from right to left gently and Izzy unconsciously leaned her body back into him. His hand shifted from the side of her waist and slid across her belly, cementing the closed proximity. His lips pressed into her lightly at first and then with a deepening hunger.

Izzy's heartbeat quickened as she reached back and clutched his thigh, raising her left hand to caress his cheek. A moan escaped her lips as the pressure on the nape of her neck intensified and jolts of pleasure electrified her body. Logan responded by inching his fingers under the edge of her shirt and pressing them against the softness of her belly.

Izzy pressed back with her hips, giving herself enough room to spin around. She wanted to look at him, to see in his eyes, and know if this was real. The gray in his eyes was more intense than she'd ever seen. He was scanning her eyes as his fingers traced her features. As if he, too, was trying to make sense of this magnetic draw. She stepped into him and moved him back against the opposing counter so that she was the one pressed into him. He curled down to meet her, brushing her hair back from her face and placing his mouth directly on hers. Her body melted into his with reactive pulses of energy reverberating the intensity of the kiss through every part of her.

The melodic trill of a cell phone erupted from the counter. It barely registered for Logan, but Izzy pulled her body away trying to locate the sound.

"Come back here." Logan softly pulled her back towards him.

"Shouldn't you get that?" Izzy asked.

Logan shook his head and nuzzled her neck.

Izzy located the culprit and moved over to pick up the phone. Logan groaned as their connection broke.

"It's your mom." Izzy held up the phone to show him the display.

"Even more reason not to answer it." Logan opted for Izzy's wrist and gently moved her closer.

Izzy lifted her eyebrows, slightly sucked in her cheeks, and hit the button connecting the call. Logan's hand whipped to his forehead, and he tilted his head back, releasing an audible sigh.

He took the phone and gave Izzy a look that made her instantly regret her impulsive decision. Maybe she could be a bit controlling—but her instincts were spot on with the reporters.

Logan went to the porch and out of earshot while Izzy served up the soup and arbitrarily determined the toppings and amounts. He still hadn't come back by the time she had put away the leftovers and lamented that the soup was already cold.

When Logan did re-enter the kitchen, his head hung low.

"Everything okay?" Izzy felt a little silly asking when the answer was so obvious.

"Well, let's see. We just chased a reporter off the porch, which at the very least cost my mother an opportunity for fame and fortune, and apparently may have also robbed her of a future daughter-in-law." Logan's face remained stern, but Izzy's shoulders fell forward as she let out an involuntary giggle.

"We aren't done yet," Logan continued. "Additionally, the Royal Order of the Rose has made the Roberts Ranch the beneficiary of their fundraising at the Labor Day Rose River Fest next weekend, and folly such as this stands to endanger all of that. Which means she'll have no choice but to meet with that snake, Declan Powers, to see how he's offering to help."

"Now, come on. That sucked, but Declan's not a snake." Izzy's eyes were endearing and with her head tilted to one side, he almost wanted to agree with anything she said. However, he was still pretty ticked she'd answered that call *and* Declan was the biggest snake he knew.

"Let's agree to disagree," Logan said the words with a thoughtful nod and moved closer towards her. "Now, where were we?"

"Don't change the subject." Izzy crossed her arms.

"Izzy, I'm grateful you brought food over, and I really enjoy your company, but let's not get into all that, 'kay? Let's celebrate you handling those reporters and how amazing you look in that color."

Her cheeks flushed at his compliment. She'd been wanting to tell him how great his hair looked short. It surprised her. She figured his untamed locks were part of what drove the ladies wild. Clean-cut Logan was impressively as alluring. She couldn't let his good looks distract her, though. That's what got you in trouble.

"You're just trying to distract me. We can have real conversations." Izzy tried to keep the teasing cadence in her words.

"I'm not saying we can't talk. These just aren't things we need to talk about right now. It's just been a hell of a week. We don't need to hash through all this. Let's just spend some time together."

"Fine, just brush me off because I say something you don't like." Izzy's voice was escalating. She wasn't even sure where all of this was coming from. "Maybe I should just go."

Logan's forehead creased, and his eyes were scanning hers, trying to interpret the situation. He finally surrendered. "That's probably best."

He leaned against the counter, propping himself up with his one good hand, and shook his head while staring at the floor.

Izzy froze for a moment and realized she had no words to say, no way to recover from all of that. She needed to leave. She briskly walked past him and let the screen door loudly creak shut behind her.

Chapter Fifteen

I zzy stayed in bed later than she stayed in bed for years. She wanted to pretend it was a luxury; not having anyone to get up and make breakfast for, but in reality, she felt restless. She kept going over the way she'd acted at Logan's the night before and being frustrated with herself. She wasn't sure if she was more upset over kissing him, answering the call from his mom, or trying to force him into a conversation that wasn't her business. Or maybe she was upset at him. He was the one who started kissing her neck and wasn't willing to talk about anything.

She also stayed in bed that long because she had no clue what to do with her time. There were so many options—it was debilitating.

It was nearly 11 by the time she got up and took a shower. Afterward, she busied herself cleaning the house and then she decided that was *not* the best use of this time. So, she made an elaborate brunch of waffles and berries with homemade chocolate sauce.

When she heard her cell phone go off a little after 1 p.m. She rushed to it; wondering if it would be Logan. She was crestfallen when it was simply one of her colleagues, Willa, inviting her to come out to Petals and Pints for dinner. She wanted Izzy to meet her best friend, Sierra, who was visiting from back east. Ordinarily, she would say no and use Marco as her excuse. Since he wasn't there, she didn't have an off-the-cuff reason. She also wondered if it might not be a good idea to get out. She clearly wasn't doing a good job of keeping herself busy while staying in. To make it a little more palatable, she asked to invite her sister Selena. That way, if Sierra was someone she had nothing in common with, Willa wouldn't be stuck in the middle bridging the gap. Luckily, Selena would be back from camping by 3 p.m., so it should work fine.

With her evening plans in place, Izzy loosened up a bit and enjoyed the afternoon. She even spent a bit of time reading a book she'd neglected on her nightstand since she unpacked from her move to Rose River. She lounged on her patio drinking lemonade, enjoying the quiet, and felt as if she was taking full advantage of her time.

When evening rolled around, Izzy took her time getting ready. She couldn't name the last time she put on lipstick and eyeliner; work didn't require such things. She had an impossible time figuring out what to wear. Most of her clothes were overly formal work attire, trying to make her look taller or more in charge, or most appropriate for frolicking in the park with a four-year-old. Not much in between. She dressed down one of her sleeveless work blouses with a pair of jeans and loosened it one button further than normal. The finishing touch was some flashy earrings she hadn't worn since her early 20s when she used to go out in LA. Overall, it pleased her how well it came together.

Getting out of her car in the Petals and Pints parking lot, Izzy turned her head to follow a wolf whistle. She laughed when she saw it was her sister, Selena.

"Look at you! I didn't think you owned anything other than mom jeans." Selena called out walking towards her.

"Well, the joke's on you then, because every pair of jeans I own are technically mom jeans."

"I can't argue with that." Selena linked her arm with Izzy's and they headed in the door. You had to walk through the bar to get to the restaurant and outside dining patio. It surprised Izzy to find the place bustling. After all, it was a Sunday night.

One head with a cowboy hat seemed to stick out in the middle of the crowd.

"Is that Logan?" Selena asked, wiggling Izzy's arm.

Izzy nodded her head, but she wasn't sure if Selena noticed the nod. She couldn't take her eyes off of Logan. He was wearing a jet black felt cowboy hat that caught the eye even more than his height did. Rose River was much more small town than cowboy country. Including the Robert's Ranch, there were only about 5 or 6 ranches or farms that stretched through the valley and into the base of the mountains. Most of what they had was logging camps up into the mountains and canneries down near the ocean.

Logan's back was leaning up against the bar and he seemed to turn every which way to accommodate the conversations.

"I know that he's kinda cute, but I don't ever remember him being so popular." Selena turned to Izzy.

"I guess losing your ranch to a wildfire moves you up the popularity scale a tad. I hope this isn't too overwhelming for him. His concussion is still healing."

"He's a big boy. He can take care of himself. He looks fine," Selena gave Izzy a bit of a shake since Izzy couldn't seem to take her eyes off Logan. "Look, there's Willa and her friend." Selena started moving Izzy in the right direction.

Izzy kept looking at Logan even as her feet followed Selena. She was hoping Logan would at least look up and catch her eye. It never happened, and she intentionally sat with her back to the bar when she joined the others at the table.

Chapter Sixteen

L ogan peeled back the edge of the label on this longneck bottle. The drink was already warm, but he was trying to nurse the same one, staving off all the attempts to buy him another round. He felt better but still needed the pain pills to sleep and could be a little unsteady on his feet. He didn't care to know the effect of a few too many beers on his current state.

Caring well-wishers engulfed them—Nate and Tony were eating it up. Every time Logan refused a drink, he referred the buyer over to them, noting the two of them were who pulled him out of the barn and drove him down the mountain.

The boys had lured him out, claiming it had been a week and everyone needed to see he was okay. He wondered if they were savvier than him and knew this would come with a significant amount of free drinks. Luckily, he drove, and he'd given them both another paid day off tomorrow. Things were still being sorted out, and he'd be working with Jake on paperwork, options, and plans.

Logan appreciated some of it. Ike Collier, an old friend of his dad's that worked in the logging camps before he retired, had bought him that first beer and told him how proud he was of him for carrying on his dad's legacy. That nearly moved him to tears. The ladies from the Royal Order of the Rose kept pushing their way through the crowd to dote on him; mostly seeking accolades for naming the Robert's Ranch the benefactor for the Rose River Fest event. He wished to his core that his mom was the only one who had to handle that, especially since she was the one that created the mess. He tried to focus on complementing the ladies. Mrs. Williams' ivory brooch of a rose was simply stunning, and Mrs. Meyer looked so young for her age! That seemed to be enough for them to miss the fact he wasn't groveling with gratitude.

Kit, well, Kit was something he could always do without. He didn't understand why she couldn't take a hint. He saw the way Tony looked at her too—killed him that Tony was genuinely interested (though Logan wouldn't wish her on anyone) and yet she clung to this imaginary relationship she had invented with Logan that didn't exist.

She was a constant buzz in the background tonight, telling everyone how terrible Logan looked when he arrived at the clinic, how she didn't know what she would do if she ever lost him. She made it sound as if they were an item, and even though it had been a decade since they were, no one seemed to remember it ever changed. Everyone only remembered things as they once were. Each time she would reach out and touch Logan's arm, he would turn away. Each time she moved closer, he would find a reason to inch in the opposite direction. He had urges to yell into the crowd, "Do y'all not realize what this woman did to me—I want *nothing* to do with her and that will never change." They all just wanted this fantasy of the Homecoming King and Queen staying in the hometown and living happily ever after.

During one of his skillful twists away from her, he caught sight of Selena, Andres' other sister, getting a tray of drinks from the bar. He caught her eye, and they both smiled and waved. He watched her walk back to a table with some other ladies he didn't know and *Izzy*. Izzy was there. He kept staring in that direction, but Izzy's back was to him and the redhead across the table from her was starting to think he was looking at her.

I zzy kept smiling and nodding at everything Sierra said. She just couldn't believe how much Sierra had to say. She didn't stop talking.

It surprised her that Willa and Sierra were best friends. They seemed so different. Sierra is a fiery, opinionated redhead who thinks the world revolves around her. Willa is a selfless giving social worker, who puts everyone else first.

Apparently, opposites attract in friendships as well as romances.

Izzy needed a break and figured going outside straight from the table was too obvious, so she opted for the ladies' room and dismissed offers of accompaniment. Fortunately, the end of the hall by the ladies' room also connects to the outdoor patio and there was an open space between the patio and parking lot.

"Ditching out on your dates, are you?"

Izzy spun around, surprised to see Logan behind her. A smile creases her lips before she put her guard up. "Only for a moment. Did you manage to escape your throngs of fans?"

"Isn't it ridiculous?" Logan sighed. "I never should have agreed to come out with Nate and Tony. I didn't expect all this."

"You're a local hero. What else would you expect? If Nate, Tony, or someone from George's Ranch had been in your situation, you'd be in line buying them beers, too."

"Logic, you're always hitting me with your logic. Not fair. I have too much going on, no room for logic." Logan looked down at the ground. His eyes were sheepish. "Speaking of which, I think I owe you an apology."

"Yeah, I am not sure which one of us needs to apologize either," Izzy lifted her shoulders in a slight shrug. "It's been a while since I've done anything like this. I may be a touch quick on the defense."

"A touch quick, and pretty damn good at it. You had me feeling guilty." Logan said.

Izzy laughed and then quickly pressed her fingers to her lips to stifle it; folks from tables looked their way.

"I'm used to knowing what is best. I guess I don't know everything about your situation.

I should probably leave room for finding that out." She shuffled her feet slightly. "In my professional life, it's best to have the fastest and strongest answer; otherwise, I get eaten alive. Fortunately, I also usually have the most information and tend to be right."

"My mom brings out the worst in me. Trust me, it's best if I prepare myself for her calls and take them as infrequently as possible."

Izzy nodded her agreement. "Is she staying in Portland for the foreseeable future?"

"Probably not. She thinks I need a press secretary."

Izzy's shoulder shook with a laugh. "Sorry, not sorry."

"Grateful, completely grateful. Let her do the interviews." Logan's eyes were lighter and more playful. Izzy had the urge to reach up and run her fingers down his arm, but she kept herself in check.

"Well, maybe we could try hanging out at my house. I promise not to answer your phone for you."

"Yeah, I'd love to spend a little more time with Marco. I've only seen him once since you guys moved back." Logan's eyes brightened.

A feeling like the first sunny day in spring washed over Izzy. It meant a lot that her son factored in without her mentioning it. "Marco is with his dad this week, so I'm afraid it'll just be me."

Logan gave her a sly wink. "I think I can handle that." They both held that moment a few seconds longer. Logan's lips were in a slight smile, and Izzy's chest flushed with anticipation.

"Why don't I bring over pizza, since you brought food last time?" Logan offered.

"That works—anything you want as long as there is no pineapple. It's an aberration to put pineapple on pizza."

Logan laughed softly. "I won't tell my mom you said that."

"What?" Izzy's eyebrows crinkled.

"Nevermind," Logan flitted the comment off with a quick gesture. "I'm guessing you're off around 5:00 p.m.? So say 6:30 p.m.? Give you time to get home and get settled?"

"Sure, that works."

"I'm looking forward to it." Logan leaned down slightly as though he might go in for a kiss, and then suddenly stood up straight, glancing around at their surroundings, and tilted his hat to her before heading back inside.

Chapter Seventeen

"I thought of you as a jock."

Logan's jaw dropped slightly at Izzy's comment. "Really? That was *it*?"

"You were my brother's friend. All you guys ever talked about was sports. That, and science, were all Andres even cared about." Izzy ate bites of pizza through her remarks, letting go of all pretenses.

"I still remember that first time I *really* noticed you, and you just thought of me as a dumb jock." Logan's voice dropped slightly. He was looking down at his plate.

"I never said I didn't think you were hot," Izzy tilted her head to the side and raised her eyebrows slightly. "What do you mean 'really' noticed me?" Izzy covered her mouth as she said the words to obscure the food she was still chewing.

"Out in the field at your parent's, you were naming the constellations."

"Oh, my gosh, that is so embarrassing! I was such a dork. I never imagined you would be out there. I was completely mortified." Izzy raised her hand to her forehead.

"You had nothing to be embarrassed about. You were cute and sweet." The right side of Logan's mouth curled up, showing a bit of his dimple.

"I was a child, totally intimidated by this gorgeous upperclassman who was talking to me when I was an awkward freshman!"

"Wait, I thought I was just some jock?" Logan squinted his eyes at her.

"Okay, so maybe when I was fourteen thinking you were some jock was more of a compliment than it is now."

Logan laughed. "I remember thinking how unique you were. How beautiful, in this way, so different from all the other girls I knew. I just didn't know what to do with that information. I mean, you were my best friend's little sister, who was barely more than a child."

"Are you sure that's me you're remembering? That sounds like an imaginary version of me. Besides, you had the perfect girlfriend. I doubt you noticed anyone else."

"I was a teenage boy. Of course, I noticed other people. I never would've done anything about it, but I wasn't blind." Logan rubbed his nose. "I think I mostly stayed with Kit because I didn't know how to break up with her. I even tried a few times, but she wasn't having that."

"Whatever happened with you two?"

"I am sure there are a million more interesting things for us to talk about." Logan pushed his chair back, grabbed the pizza box, stacked his plate on top, and went into the kitchen. He added from a safe distance, "Unless you are ready for me to ask questions about Marco's dad."

"Hard pass. Dishes are a good idea." Izzy got up and followed him.

After the dishes were done, Izzy turned from the sink and lifted her hands. "Now what?"

A sly grin moved across Logan's lips as he walked slowly to her. He lifted her right hand and gently kissed her palm. He ran his lips along the hollow near her thumb before wrapping his lips in the gap between her thumb and forefinger and gently pulling. Her body reacted instantly, and she reached back to grasp the counter. He continued a trail of small kisses down her arm, holding her gaze. When he got to her elbow, he lifted his head away and gently led her into the front room.

Logan sat on the couch, and his steely eyes beckoned her to sit as close as possible. They awkwardly fell into each other like two teenagers. Trying to smoothly maneuver around Logan's cast elicited playful giggles. They finally eased into a position, leaning back with Izzy somewhat on top of him. He tilted his head, parting his lips to brush softly against hers. He tightened his grip around her waist, pulling her body closer to his. His kisses intoxicated her. It had been so long since she'd felt anything like this that it was dizzying—tasting him, feeling her body respond to him. His left hand slipped from her waist, up the bare flesh just under the edge of her shirt, sending a thrill straight down to her toes. As his fingers trailed further up along her back, the gooseflesh spread down her arms.

She fumbled with the edge of his shirt, pulling it up; wanting to feel his bare skin. She pulled her body back enough to slide in one hand and ran her fingers along his smooth and defined chest. Her fingers spread across the tight muscles and then traced up his taut shoulder.

Under her thigh, she felt the vibrating of his phone. She tried ignoring it and focused on the pressure of his kiss, the warmth of his tongue. It wasn't long before the vibrating stopped, only to start again a few moments later.

Izzy pulled back from him. "I get it. I'm not supposed to answer your phone, so I won't. But this is really distracting."

"I tried to help by putting it on silent."

"I know." She slid against the back of the couch, away from him.

"I'll see what it's about." Logan fished the phone from his pocket. "How surprising, it's my mom. I'll be right back."

Logan shifted the rest of the way out from under Izzy and walked into the next room.

Izzy smoothed her clothes and sat herself up on the couch. It was strange to be in this house experiencing these things. It was adding a new depth to her time in Rose River. A depth she didn't expect, and one she certainly welcomed.

It just seemed sudden. Certainly unexpected.

She was chewing her nails when Logan came back in.

"She has a peach cobbler and ice cream, and is expecting me at the house shortly." Logan lifted his hands with a slight shrug. "Sorry, I couldn't come up with a good reason I couldn't go home.

There is a very good reason. I just didn't quite know how to tell her."

Izzy smiled and bit her bottom lip. Mostly she understood what he was saying, but part of her wished it was easier. She knew very well if Andres had called—she couldn't explain to him why she wouldn't want to come over for dessert.

"What about Friday night?" Izzy offered. "Picnic down at the beach?"

"I'd love that, but can I bring the picnic?" Logan asked.

"You were the one that brought pizza tonight."

"I know, but it wasn't impressive. I want to be impressive." Logan's eyes danced with mischief.

"Okay, I'll bring the blanket and plates and wine. You bring the food." Izzy got to her feet and walked Logan to the door.

"I'll take it." Logan paused in front of the door and held her eyes. He wished more than anything he had two good arms with which to embrace her. He hated that it felt a little clumsy.

Izzy seemed to read his mind and closed the distance between them with her own body, wrapping her arms around him placing her head on his chest. Logan stroked her hair and pressed his lips against the top of her head. "I had a great time tonight."

"As did I." Izzy pulled back slightly and lifted her face towards his. He leaned further down to her until their lips gently connected.

There was no way that peach cobbler was better than this.

Chapter Eighteen

L ogan sifted through the contents of the picnic basket one more time. He thought it would be difficult to sneak the basket past his mom, but she was engaged on the phone in the kitchen long enough he got it from the hall closet and into his truck without her noticing. He'd bit his tongue all day. It was very tempting to ask her what one would take on a picnic to the beach. She would have the perfect answer. But she would also get nosey and be on to him. Fortunately Gina, at the deli she was the namesake and owner of, was a huge help. He'd expected something along the lines of sandwiches, but apparently, there were far more romantic foods for such occasions. He had left with various cheeses from gouda to brie, crackers, fresh crusty bread, grapes, something called Marcona Almonds, a tapenade, and a local smoked salmon dip. It all looked delicious to him. He just hoped it was enough to be considered a meal.

He got down from his truck and scanned the parking lot for Izzy's little hybrid car. He didn't get over three feet before he ran into Mr. Connor, who was there with his daughter, Liz. He endured small talk while his eyes roamed the parking lot. Everyone was so curious about the fire, but it was the last thing on earth Logan wanted to talk about. Before long, Nate's mom came strolling up, asking about his injuries and making a bigger deal out of everything. He started to think his mom's idea of leaving Rose

River wasn't such a bad idea. He hated being the center of every conversation.

Finally, he got a glimpse of Izzy's little blue car pulling into the lot. He suddenly realized that eating a meal in public, even if it was just at Otter Beach, was going to be more complicated than he'd taken the time to consider. He already had everyone in Rose River talking about the fire and his injuries. Did he also need them speculating about his personal life? He wasn't even ready to tell his mom, or an even more complicated audience, Andres, that he was interested in Izzy. Did he need rumors circulating about them before he even knew what they were?

It got cool at night on the beach, so Logan was wearing a long sleeve collared shirt. At this moment, the heat under his collar and the perspiration forming under his arms made it a poor choice. Before Izzy's car was fully parked, Logan said his goodbyes and made a hasty retreat to his truck. He whipped out his phone and sent a text, hoping to catch Izzy before she got out of her car.

Do you know
Baron's Cliff?

Izzy had her car door open when she heard
her phone ding in her purse. She quickly
grabbed it. She was much more attentive to
her phone when Marco was away. She'd spoken
to him each night before he went to bed, but
she was in constant anticipation of something
going wrong. It surprised her that the text was
from Logan, who she'd seen across the parking
lot when she'd pulled in.

Of course. Why?

The dots on the screen showed he was
preparing a reply.

Too many people
here. Let's meet
up there.

Izzy craned her head to see where he parked and noticed the backup lights were on. It seemed he wasn't waiting for an answer. She got back into her car and followed him out of the lot.

Baron's Cliff was only 10 minutes up the road, an easy drive. The complicated part was parking. It wasn't a designated landmark, more of a place locals knew about where you hopped the barrier of Hwy. 101. This meant there was only space to park two cars off the road safely. Fortunately, no one else was there, and they were both able to swing their vehicles into the available spots.

Izzy had a wary eye on Logan when she got out of her car. The sudden change of location came across as strange. Was he embarrassed to be seen with her? Was there someone else he had an eye on and they were there?

His bright smile quickly melted any questions she harbored. He hurried out of his truck and walked triumphantly to her, presenting the basket that held their dinner for the evening. She laughed at his bravado and they embraced in a lingering hug that ended with him placing a soft kiss on her forehead.

She walked to her trunk to pull out the items she'd brought and marveled they had yet to say a word and it felt so comfortable.

They didn't need to say anything.

He helped her over the barrier and they trudged through the knee-high grass and weeds to cross through the firs towards the cliffs.

Izzy's breath caught in her chest as the ocean came into full view. She'd been to Otter Beach a few times with Marco to play in the sand since she'd moved back. It was also a place they frequented on their visits to grammy's. She hadn't been up here since she was in high school. It seemed she lacked the capacity to appreciate its splendor at that stage in her life.

The waves crackled and roared against the rocks with such fervor they washed away her very thoughts. The jagged edges of where the mountains met the sea were littered with every shade of green from the majestic firs and pines that lived on the ocean's edge to moss, lichen, algae, and defiant grasses. It felt as though you could feel mother earth breathing. The ocean, too, had hints of green blooming from its deep shades of aqua that melted into the intense blue of midnight as it stretched towards the horizon. Izzy inhaled the pungent saltiness and felt the light mist on her skin. The kiss of the sea was everywhere up here.

Logan took her hand and led her supportively down through the spots where the rocks caused her feet to scramble. He had the basket in the crook of his right elbow held a little better in place because of the positioning of the cast's hard edge. When they came to a small clearing for their blanket, he sat down the basket and wrapped his arms around her, as best he could.

"Welcome home," he whispered in her ear.

The heaviness in Izzy's chest was her heart being the fullest it had ever felt. There were flutters in her belly—reminding her how scary it was to feel like this. Remembering how far you could fall when you let your heart get this high. Her head and heart were poised for a battle, but she wasn't having it. She let herself lean into Logan's broad chest and exhaled. These were the moments she wanted. This was what she wanted, *he* was what she wanted.

Chapter Nineteen

I zzy stretched her body and curled her arm back under the pillow. Her lips parted in an involuntary yawn and she debated whether to open her eyes. She felt a slight throbbing in her right temple and vaguely remembered the wine from the night before and the romantic picnic on the cliffs with Logan. As she savored the details of the evening, she felt an arm wrap around her waist and quickly covered her lips to stifle her gasp as her eyes sprung open.

Her thoughts quickly spun forward to the end of that amazing night and here she was at Logan Roberts' home, in Logan Roberts' bed, sleeping next to (and now in the arms of) the sultry cowboy himself; Logan Roberts. Izzy was a little shocked by herself. This was not how she expected the evening to have ended. Everything felt so natural and comfortable with Logan. It was like they'd been with each other for an eternity rather than a flirtation that had simply started weeks ago. She guessed that came with knowing each other since they were kids. Before she put much further thought into it, she felt Logan's lips pressing into her neck and the electricity tickling down her spine.

"Good morning, sunshine." Logan swept her hair from her face and feathered his fingers through it. "You hungry?"

Izzy's belly growled, almost as if in response to the question. Logan chuckled under his breath. "Well, I guess I better get to it." Logan swung his feet out of the bed, threw on shorts, and was out of the room before Izzy processed anything.

Izzy sat up slowly, tugged at her ear a moment, and smoothed her hair. They had decided not to drink the wine at the cliffs, since they both needed to drive home. It was after the sunset and almost time for Marco to call when Logan suggested going back to his place. Get out of the wind, a quiet place for the call, and they could finish the wine. It wasn't long before there was an invitation to stay. Without Marco being home, she had no reason not to. After all, she had stayed there before and there was a guest room. She touched her lips lightly and realized how each little decision fell like dominos to this moment.

She wrapped herself in a shirt she grabbed from Logan's closet and followed her trail of clothes that led to the stairs. She tittered with a small laugh as she gathered them all up and took them into the master bath to put herself together. After that first morning in his kitchen, she'd feel better fully dressed even if he was only wearing shorts. Her skin glowed and her eyes shone. Being impulsive and taking risks looked good on her. She twisted her hair up, but she couldn't get it to hold and decided she would let it fall around her shoulders.

She quickly made up the bed, but she left Logan's clothes littered on the floor. The smell of bacon was wafting up the stairs and beckoning her to follow. The wood steps were cool on her bare feet and the stair rail smooth under her fingers. Logan's buttery voice drifted up the stairs and a goofy grin crossed her lips as she recognized he was singing the lyrics from "She's Everything" and the country station was his subtle accompaniment.

"Hey, sunshine." Logan's singing abruptly dropped as she turned the corner.

"Is that going to become a thing?" she asked.

"What you don't like my singing?" Logan cocked his head to the side.

"No, the singing is great. I'm curious about the sunshine."

A grin spread across his face. "Do you have a more accurate term?"

"I didn't say I didn't like it. I was just curious." Izzy trailed her hand along his back as she brushed past him towards the coffee. "Where's the mugs?"

"Here, I'll get ya one. Much easier when you're taller." Logan stretched above her and Izzy ran her hand down his bare chest, thinking he was either brave or stupid to be cooking greasy bacon with so much skin exposed. She ran a finger along the edge of his waistband, and Logan's feet teetered slightly as he instinctively responded to the light touch.

A bang on the door followed by incessant attacks on the doorbell shocked his body straight, and they both looked at each other.

"Reporters again?" Izzy guessed.

Logan's eyebrows went up to concede the point, but before he could even speak, the answer came cutting through.

"Logan, sweetheart! Grab the door! I forgot my key."

Logan's jaw fell open.

Izzy's eyes widened.

Belle Roberts was making an unannounced appearance and, thank goodness, had forgotten her key.

"Logan, dear, don't make me go hunt around my car for it." Belle pressed the buzzer in rapid succession again.

"You have to go." Logan shut the cupboard and started directing Izzy's shoulders towards the back of the house.

"I'm sure she's already seen my car. My sandals are by the front door." Izzy tried slowing the steps, but Logan was moving her quickly.

"I'll grab your purse. Your sandals are too risky." Logan stopped pushing, quickly darted around the corner into the front room, grabbed her purse, and ran back to her.

Izzy stayed in place with her arms limp at her sides and a stony expression. "I can't go home barefoot."

"It's perfectly safe to drive barefoot," Logan put Izzy's purse on his arm with the cast and shifted her by the shoulder, using his good arm. "I promise I'll get your shoes back to you."

Izzy's lips moved, but they could not form words.

He was kicking her out.

This was awkward for everyone, but throwing her out the back door like she was trash?

"I'm so sorry." Logan was opening the back door and put Izzy's purse against her stomach, her arms reflexively closed around it. A quick peck on the cheek and the door was closed.

She watched him rush back down the hall and it was like she'd never been there at all.

Chapter Twenty

Logan couldn't believe he forgot his mom was coming into town for the Rose River Fest over the long weekend. The last week had been a blur, with appointments and everyone throwing the need for decisions at him. He couldn't believe it was already Labor Day Weekend. All he'd been thinking about was getting to Friday and the picnic with Izzy.

He pulled into the parking lot down by the river and it impressed him that so many people were already there. It usually wasn't until late afternoon that things picked up, especially with the carnival games lasting late into the evening. He chuckled at Izzy's sandals sitting on his front seat. He'd snuck them out in a grocery bag, and his mom hadn't even questioned it. She did comment on the car parked outside. He said it was probably just somebody taking pictures of the damage from the fire. Belle had no further questions after that.

He sent a text to Izzy thanking her for an amazing night and promising her that bacon breakfast another day, but he'd heard nothing in return. She was probably having a busy morning herself. He wondered if he should carry the sandals around in case he ran into her. In the end, he hopped down, figuring it was a good excuse to bring her back to the truck and sneak in a kiss.

Man, that woman's lips. It had been a while, but he was pretty sure if the last woman he dated kissed like that; he wouldn't be single.

He lowered his hat a bit and hunched his shoulders, keeping his head steadily turned in the opposite direction when he passed the booth for the Royal Order of the Rose. Not that he didn't appreciate them. What they were doing was amazing—the money they raised this weekend was going to bridge the large gap until the insurance money came in and he could rebuild. He just wasn't one to be the center of attention, and he wasn't sure about how to express his gratitude. He knew his mom was doing a lot to show appreciation, but he wish he had ideas of how to convey that when his words came up short.

Walking away from the booths and towards the carnival games, Logan thought he glimpsed a ripple of Izzy's dark hair across the fairway. He squinted his eyes and looked a little closer. That couldn't possibly be her. This woman was with another guy. The guy was pretty ordinary; polo shirt, khaki shorts, mousy brown hair cut short; it must be another woman wandering the fair with her husband. The woman touched the guy's back, affirming his hypothesis.

When he turned to walk the other way, the couple moved towards the prizes, and Logan recognized the curve of her impish nose. *It was Izzy.* Logan's teeth clenched and his muscles tightened; starting at his neck and moving down his back.

⁓ele⁓

Izzy was still stomping her feet three hours later. He had the *audacity* to send her home barefoot! She had done the walk of shame a few times in college, but it was never like this. Apparently, those college boys were more respectful than this grown man she *thought* she was falling for. She inhaled deeply and closed her eyes as she breathed out. She only had a few more hours until Marco was coming home, and she needed to focus on that. She laid one hand on her chest and the other on her belly. One more deep inhale, smoothed her T-shirt, and walked over to the little booth the clinic had set up.

"Hey, Raya. How's it been going?" Izzy instinctively straightened the pamphlets on the table and ran her fingers over the cloth.

"Pretty good," Raya responded. "It was a great idea to have fresh fruit for the kids instead of candy. They also love these fidget toys, even if they're gonna break within a week. You had great ideas."

"Thanks. I appreciate hearing that." Izzy's stiff shoulders relaxed. "I haven't been to this festival since I was in high school, so it took a bit of effort to remember the setup. And with kids these days, you never know what might be a good idea. I was nervous I wouldn't hit the mark."

"Spot on, as always." Dr. Carrington walked up from behind and squeezed her shoulder.

She reached up and lightly touched his hand before he moved it away. "Hey, why the long face? Missing your boy? Earlier this week, you seemed on cloud nine. I thought you were enjoying some time to yourself."

"So did I." Izzy mumbled under her breath, "He'll be back in a couple of hours. I'm only checking in here before heading over to my mom's place. Do you need anything?"

Raya smiled and shook her head.

"Let me know if that changes." Izzy turned to leave when Dr. Carrington caught her hand.

"Hey, I miss my wife like crazy most days. I know how it feels." Dr. Carrington gave her hand a little squeeze.

Izzy's cheeks burned slightly, and she curled her free hand around her middle. His wife was halfway around the world serving as a doctor for the Naval base in Saipan with hardly any leave—and she had him tending to her because she walked barefoot this morning.

"Dr. Carrington, it must be so hard. I'm sorry that I get so wrapped up in my own—"

"We aren't at the clinic. Call me Greg here."

"Greg, I'm sorry. What can I do for you?" She emphasized the last word with a sharp point to his chest.

Greg chortled. Most people laugh. Greg chortled.

"How about you help me win her a teddy bear, and while we are at it, we can win one for Marco as well."

"Sounds like a plan." Izzy looped her arm in Greg's and they headed off to the carnival games.

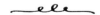

Logan's feet froze. Every muscle had tensed in succession. He couldn't take his eyes off of them. His heart was pounding. He took a hard step in their direction.

"Oh, there you are, dear." Belle had left her apartment in the city at 5:00 a.m. to drive down to Rose River, and yet she looked fresh as a daisy kissed by the morning dew. She'd tucked her blonde hair neatly up in a chignon, and although she was wearing sensible flats, her suit jacket was much too warm for this weather. "I was looking all over for you. The ladies at the Royal Order of the Rose are dying to chat with you. I was telling them all about the fact we are selling the land. They find that so fascinating. Especially since the original intent of this weekend's funds was to tide the ranch over until the insurance settlement came in to rebuild."

Belle paused for a moment, giving Logan the opportunity to respond.

His mind was only grinding gears. Logan's eyes were still glued on Izzy and this mystery man. And yet, his mother's announcement they were selling the property had sparked a fire in his belly.

Hearing no immediate response, Belle continued, "So, if we were to do that, then we would just use the money to repair the barn, right? Or prepare the property for sale? Moving expenses? With Declan's generous—"

"Declan? What's Declan got to do with any of this?" There was an intensity in Logan's voice that slowly lost its venom as he finished the question.

"Why, he is the one offering you nearly a half-million dollars for that half charred property of ours."

"Since when? And not to me, to you perhaps, but mama you don't own that property." Logan's left hand was balled into a fist and there was a steady ache in his right arm as the muscles tightened around the bones wanting to do the same.

Belle's mouth dropped open, "Well, I—"

"Mama, I'm not trying to be sharp, but that nice apartment you live in is because of that ranch. You may think a half-million is a lot of money, but we clear nearly one-fifth of that in profit every year. Dad set up good relationships with breeding horses and that brings in a lot more than the cattle ever have. I love that ranch. I got hurt saving those horses, and I'm keeping it. I know I can't run the ranch forever. I paid the place off, and I'm saving up accordingly. If those horses weren't worth so damn much; we wouldn't even have insurance on the place."

Belle shuffled her feet slightly and adjusted her sleeves. Logan wasn't sure what to do. He'd never rendered his mom speechless before.

Logan softened his tone and took his mom's hand. "Mom, I appreciate everything you are doing. The money from the Royal Order of the Rose is the only way I can keep paying Nate and Tony or start clearing the debris. It will also mean I can pay back some of the savings I'm already using to keep things afloat, and that can go to my medical bill." Logan lifted his cast, and they both gave a partial smile that revealed where Logan got his dimple from. "Do what you are amazing at. Talk to the ladies, talk to the reporters, but please don't sell my ranch out from under me."

"It's not like I signed anything." Belle playfully swatted at her son, "But seriously, please come say hello and clear up this mess I've been making."

Logan gently nods. He glanced back and no longer saw Izzy. He winced at the implications of what he'd seen and turned to follow his mom in the other direction.

Chapter Twenty-one

"Can I name him? Can I name him?" Marco bounced up and down like the front room rug was a trampoline.

"Of course, you can name him. He's yours." Izzy tried to catch Marco's shoulder, but it was futile. She'd seen the ring of ice cream and chocolate on his lips. This was a recently induced sugar high. *Thanks, Victor.* "I wanna hear about your trip. Come sit down." She modeled the movement and patted the seat.

"It was boring. I told you everything." Marco inhaled another breath. "Each night on the phone."

"Come sit." There was a sharpness to her tone, so she softly added, "your mom missed you."

Marco came to the couch and leaned up against his mom. She draped her arms around him and felt his rapid heartbeat. She pressed the length of his arms to calm him.

"Okay." Marco's body sprang straight up. "Is that enough?"

"Fine." Izzy dropped her arms and released a deep breath.

It pleased Izzy the bouncing had stopped, but he was twirling the bear in circles by its arms.

"When are we going to the fair?" Marco lifted his arms to twirl his body as well. "Do I get to ride the horses?"

"We've talked about the horses. You're still too little for the horses."

"Dad says I'm big now,"—Marco's twirling came to an abrupt stop—"Dad would let me ride the horses."

Izzy tucked her hands under her legs and pressed down on them when she leaned forward. "You aren't with dad right now, you're with me. When you're with me, you follow my rules, understand?"

Marco's eyes were big, and he nodded slowly.

"If you say anything like that again tonight, we will leave the fair and you won't get to go back." Izzy bore into Marco's eyes. Her heart was racing and tears were prickling the back of her eyes. She swiped at her cheek. "Now, put away bear so we can go."

———

YOU HERE YET?

Izzy sent her sister the text before she got Marco out of the car. She could use a friendly face tonight. She wondered if it was safe to tell Selena about everything that was happening with Logan and the ridiculous stunt he pulled this morning. Just thinking about it made her teeth clench.

Her phone went off as they were entering the booth area.

DRIVING BE THERE
IN 5 ME AT PIGS?

Izzy stared at the words. 'Me at pigs?' it made no sense. Oh—speech to text. *Meet* at pigs. That worked. She figured it was safer to head in that direction and have Selena figure it out when she arrived.

Izzy's phone dinged again. She rolled her eyes at her sister's disregard for safety.

CAN WE TALK?

This one was from Logan. He had already sent her three texts today, but she ignored them all. She just didn't know how to respond to him. It may be a little premature to block him. Eventually, she wanted her sandals back. She tucked her phone back into her pocket.

The animals were in a field up away from the river and the carnival games. A bit of a walk, but they were easy to find. Finding the pigs particularly was a little more difficult. There were bunnies, sheep, and everything else you could imagine. She finally stopped someone.

"Can you tell us where the pigs are?"

"Pigs?" The girl had her hair up in braids and seemed to wear a jacket that indicated she belonged and was a caretaker of animals here.

"Yeah. This is the area with the animals. Aren't their pigs around here somewhere?"

"Oh, no." The girl scrunched up her face as if this question had been absurd. "There used to be a long time ago, but it's a short fair and they make too big of a mess."

"Oh. Thanks."

Great. Now what? Izzy pulled out her phone to text Selena and felt Marco tugging at the edge of her jean shorts.

"Mom, look! The horses, there's the horses!" Marco's feet were shuffling in place, but his tug was going at full tilt.

"That's great, bud. I just gotta text Selena and tell her there are no pigs."

"Can we wait for her by the horses?" Marco's bounce had begun.

"Sure, after I finish this text." Izzy found it hard to write a text while being swayed side to side by the power of a four-year-old, but she managed. When she relented, he'd pulled her shoulder to a mere three feet off the ground as he hastened their way to the corrals.

They finally found enough of a break where they could get glimpses of the ring. It looked like a bunch of horses pinned together, and some of them weren't happy to be there.

"That's the broncs. They'll be riding them later." A gentleman to her left shared unsolicited. She smiled and nodded and moved Marco a little further in the other direction to find a break in the crowd. She was doing her best to keep a hand on his shoulder as Marco ducked and shuffled, trying to get the best view.

"Izzy Morales, well, I'll be. How long has it been?" Declan Powers was wearing a polo shirt, which seemed a little out of place next to the cowboy hats and jeans down at the corrals. But his green eyes were bright, his smile was beaming, and save the crook in his nose, he looked about the same as he did in high school.

"Hey, Declan, it has been a long time. I don't think I've seen you since I moved back."

"You moved back? Weren't you in LA? That's exciting." Declan's head nodded with his words as if he was giving his approval, even though he was asking her the questions.

"Yeah. And I brought someone with me." Izzy turned and pointed to Marco, who had snaked another foot beyond her reach.

"That's just great. How old is he?" Declan's head continued to nod.

"Four, but he thinks he's 14 already." Izzy moved closer to Marco and punctuated her words with glances back towards him.

"I hear you're out there saving the day." Declan leaned in closer and moved with her.

"What?" Izzy craned her neck to hear better.

"Aren't you the one that drove Logan up to the hospital in Junction City?"

Now Izzy's head nodded. She threw her arms up. "Guilty as charged." She didn't understand why she was being so animated. It was always uneasy talking to someone you hadn't seen in a long time.

"Well, I'm not nearly the Saint you are, but I'm helping in my way. I'm buying the place."

Izzy's feet froze. She blinked her eyes hard. "What do you mean buy the place?"

"I'm buying it. Even in its terrible burned-up condition. Helping them get out from under it."

Izzy's mouth was dry. "I didn't know they were trying to get out from under it."

"Yeah, I guess Logan wants to go back to school—some program in Portland."

Izzy could hear her heartbeat in her ears. It was loud and slowing by the second. She swayed slightly.

A stranger next to her braced her arm. He said something, but he had to repeat it before it registered. "Hey, isn't that your kid?"

Izzy rocked back on her heels, spinning to where Marco was last standing. She saw his legs squeezing in an army crawl under the fence.

Chapter Twenty-two

L ogan kept pulling his hat, raking his fingers through his hair, and putting it back on. He'd been walking around this fair for what seemed like an eternity. He tried to leave after he spent some time wooing the ladies at the table for the Royal Order of the Rose but had seen Izzy's car in the parking lot. She wasn't returning his texts, and he didn't know what to do about it.

He didn't want to charge halfcocked into a situation, but he felt like he deserved an explanation. They hadn't talked about being exclusive, but they were adults, and she certainly made it sound like he was the only thing holding her interest.

He'd walked up and down around the carnival games, and couldn't bear that loop again. He got stopped every two feet with some well-intending comment or question. He decided to head over to the corral and see if one of the guys were free to grab a bite to eat. If nothing else, he'd feel more at home with the horses and it would give him a chance to clear his mind.

As the corrals came into view, he instantly picked Izzy out of the crowd. It's as though her aura was drawing him. Something about her miraculously made the short gal with long hair the one that was easy to find in a crowd.

His nostrils flared when he realized she was with someone. The guy seemed taller, but it was probably the tilt of the ground. Logan rubbed the back of his neck. This must be why she wasn't answering any of his texts. He kicked at the dirt in front of him, measuring his next move when both Izzy and the guy shifted when she turned to look at something. That was when he saw the face. Declan Powers. Of all the guys in Rose River, she was snuggling up and spending her day with Declan Powers? Logan's breathing became shallow and his jaw tensed. His left hook may not be as good as his right, but Declan may just get another notch in his nose.

His steps were heavy and deliberate as he closed the space between them. When he was still a stone's throw away, Izzy called out Marco's name and flung herself towards the ground, aiming at the base of the corral. Every hair on Logan's body stood on end. He rushed to the closest break in the crowd and, without even further assessing the situation, he clumsily scaled the fence using his elbow where his useful right hand should be. The horses were in a frenzy and he spotted Marco tucked up close to the fence near the gate, his body shaking with fear or likely sobs.

Logan moved slowly. Calming these horses was the first thing he needed to figure out. He slid his cast behind his back, knowing it would be sure to spook them. He loosened his stance—a slight bend at the knee, arm stretched out—and down, elbow loose, slightly crouched. He lowered his voice to the tone that worked on the hundreds of horses he'd charmed over his lifetime. He knew to stay where they could see him. He knew there was one he had to soothe first to get the rest to follow. He had his match in this one. He was a fiery bronc. A Chestnut Arabian with something to prove.

Their eyes locked, and Logan moved closer. The bucking ceased, yet he flared his nostrils and pawed the ground. When he'd stopped bucking, the other horses running amok had done the same. Logan kept his eyes connected to the Chestnut Arabian. With Marco in his side view, he walked a delicate grapevine, keeping even with the horse, and getting closer to the post where Marco had fixed himself.

Tears streamed down Izzy's face and streaked a path through the dust that was now covering every bit of her. She was begging Marco to come to her, but he'd balled up and she wasn't sure he could hear her over the crowd and his crying. They designed the corral to keep people out, so nothing more than a wiry four-year-old could squeeze through the gaps in the metal. Her fingers barely reached him and her hand alternated between pulling on him and trying to soothe him with her touch. In the background, the din would ebb and flow. The fury of the horses is what she was closest to. Behind that, there was a symphony of murmurs that burst into a low roar. The shift in the crowd had her hoping they were finding a way to get her baby out. She couldn't check for sure—she would never again take her eyes off of Marco.

G etting Marco would take two arms, and two arms would mean wielding his cast. Logan needed a swift escape. There was a gate near to where Marco was, but he had no idea how to operate it and they could both be trampled before his one good hand figured it out. He took his eyes off the Chestnut Arabian for a moment to get a full look at the gate versus assessing it in his side vision. His skin tingled with goose flesh.

He appreciated Nate, but he'd never been so happy to see him. Nate was straddling the top of the corral, making it clear he had his eye on Logan and his hand on the gate. The Chestnut Arabian reared back, not in a buck, but a defiant show that he knew Logan was up to something. Logan weighed his options; get Marco and get out as fast as possible, or soothe the bronc further, move slowly, and exit with grace.

He inched closer to the bronc with his hand down. It got him further away from Marco, but this horse needed reassurance. There was deep red in the chestnut's hue and his eyes were dark as coal, further highlighted by the dark color surrounding them. Muscle twisted around every inch of his body and the glint in his eye showed his pride. No one could tame him.

Much to Logan's surprise, his soft words and slow approach enthralled the beast, and he took steps towards Logan. When he was close enough, Logan reached for his chin and after initially pulling back, he laid his muzzle back in Logan's hand when it remain unmoved. Logan held his hand steady and then gave one gradual firm stroke, following the curve of the horse's jaw. As he reached the end and his hand slipped away from the Chestnut Arabian, the bronc seemed to nod and turned to wander with the other horses.

Logan knew not to move too quickly, but also knew this was his shot. He still walked backward, keeping his eye on the herd, but this time at a steady clip. He crumpled in front of Marco at an odd angle, still trying to be his shield. He reached back and gently brushed his hand against his leg—near to Izzy's.

Izzy gasped and moved her hand to touch Logan's. Tears shone in her eyes, and in the glance that Logan took in, he also saw the radiating warmth of gratitude.

"Marco, hey guy," Logan wasn't sure Marco heard him over the tumult of the horses, crowd, and Marco's heaving sobs. "I'm gonna get you out of here. I just need you to trust me."

Logan paused a moment, hoping Marco would respond.

Logan's palms were slick with perspiration, and his heart was racing. The horses would soon realize that the addition of this kid was upping the ante for him, too. Logan twisted to the left, scooping him with his good arm and leaning in with his chest to sandwich Marco in tight. He heard the sharp cry Marco made when he pressed him into place and Logan's chest caved at the idea he may have added to the child's pain.

Logan's cast was out in front on full display, almost a shield, though the horses surely saw it as a battling rod. The muscles tightened in his torso as he made his way towards the gate with purpose.

This movement fully churned the broncs.

Logan kept his eye on the gate, though his peripheral vision was ablaze with moving figures and hooves volleying into the air. Logan felt something closing in on him and braced the child closer.

The Chestnut Arabian was flanking his left side. He'd come to their aid and was running alongside to create a barrier between them and the other frenzied horses.

Nate flicked open the gate right as they reached it and Logan slid through.

Logan's chest was heaving. His head felt light. But he needed to get this boy to his mom. They circled the corral, pushing through the crowd. Logan lifted Marco a little higher and felt his body slacken. "You're okay, boy. We got you out. Just getting to your mom."

Marco was still crying, but they were sniffles and light sobs versus the gut-wrenching wails that consumed him in the corral. He reached his arms up and encircled Logan's neck.

Izzy finally pushed her way through the crowd and Logan dropped to his knees so that Izzy could easily access her son.

"Marco, oh my god, Marco, are you okay?" Izzy wrapped herself around both of them with her head nuzzled in close. Marco lifted his head and shook it no.

"What is it, what hurts?" Izzy unfurled Marco, investigating the fresh scrapes on his dirt marred skin and looking for anything more serious.

"My leg, I hurt my leg." Marco erupted with a loud wail and grasped his right leg. Izzy tried gentle touches, stern words, and every which way to gain access to the leg, but Marco wasn't having it.

She finally threw her arms up.

"I don't think he's going to die, but can you carry him to my car? Maybe my brother can have more luck with him."

Nate's voice came out of the crowd. "I'll call Andres."

Logan's head spun towards him. "Thank you, Nate. I owe you." Nate gave him a thumbs up and pulled out his cell.

Marco settled in, almost sitting on Logan's cast with his arms around his neck.

"Do you think he's just doing this for the ride?" Izzy's creases of concern framed her eyes. The tangles in her hair and dirt on her face made it look like she was coming out of a war zone.

"It's okay either way, I don't mind."

Chapter Twenty-three

Logan kept twisting his hat in his hands and folding the crease on the top. He occasionally glanced at the door and wondered if he should leave. Elena is the only other one in the lobby.

"I hear you're the one who rescued my grandson."

Logan bowed his head slightly and didn't know what to say. He wasn't sure if the guy with the cast going in was the best idea. There was a moment he wasn't sure they were making it out okay.

"I'll go check on things. Maybe Izzy can give you an update." Elena laid her hand on Logan's shoulder a moment before she walked back into the abyss of the clinic.

Logan's leg jostled up and down. He couldn't stop fidgeting. He had so much to try to not think about. He saw Izzy walk through the door immediately rose to his feet. He was so unsure of where things were at with them, but seeing her glassy eyes and the remnants of her tears, his feet nearly leaped across the room to be next to her.

"Hey, how are things going back there?" Logan stuck his hat back on his head and wrapped his free hand around her.

Izzy collapsed into his embrace and released a breath held deep in her belly.

"He broke his leg. Can you believe that?" She stretched her face as she wiped under her eye. "It's a broken tibia-fibula, Andres isn't worried about it and thinks he'll heal up just fine. He doesn't have any acute trauma to the outside of his leg, so they didn't trample him or anything. Probably got it stuck in the wrong position when he was trying to get away from them."

Logan still wasn't clear about how Marco got into the corral. He knew little ones got away quick, and he didn't want to say anything that would open the door for her questioning herself.

"Hey, what's this I hear about you moving to Portland?" Izzy tried to sound casual, but her voice had gone up an octave in the middle and she was drawing circles on his chest with her finger.

"What?" Logan pulled back from her and gently titled her chin up.

"Declan said you were moving."

"Oh, he would like that, wouldn't he?" Logan took a step back and could feel the rush of blood in his veins. "Why are you hanging out with him?"

"I wasn't I just ran into him five minutes before Marco crawled in with the horses." Izzy wrapped her arms around her and shifted her weight back towards her heels.

"You were with him at the carnival games earlier, too,"

"What? Are you stalking me?" Izzy's chin jutted out.

Logan exhaled and let his shoulders slacken. "It sure sounds like that, doesn't it?"

"I was with Dr. Carrington, if you must know, helping him pick out a carnival prize for his *wife* and letting him win a bear for Marco."

Logan's head hung down, and he shrugged slightly. "Guess I'm not good at this 'huh?"

"No, you're not, but before we go there, what's your deal with Declan?"

Logan took his hat off, ran his fingers through his hair, and then tossed his hat on the nearest chair. He squared his shoulder, bit his lip, and let the truth flow. "You know that hitch in his nose?"

"I noticed that."

"That's my fault."

Izzy flinched, "Logan! I can't believe you'd do something like that."

"I wouldn't. At least not now. It was stupid. It was a decade ago, but my dad had just died and then I-I found him... Well, let's just say he's the reason I finally got to break up with Kit."

Izzy gasped and flung her hand to her mouth. No wonder he was keeping a bit too close of an eye on her.

That wasn't his biggest problem, though.

"Do you realize how badly you insulted and humiliated me this morning?" Izzy pulled her shoulders back looking him square in the eye.

Logan tilted his head to the side and rubbed his chin. He did *not,* in fact, realize that.

But he was pretty sure that was not the right answer.

"I've got some work to do, don't I?" Logan dropped his hands in surrender.

"You should be proud you are with me." Izzy choked slightly on the words.

"Oh, Izzy," Logan scooped her up and pulled her close. "I am, I am in awe of the fact I get to be with you,"—he tilted her head back slightly—"I swear this morning was saving you from my mom; not the other way around."

Izzy nuzzled her head into his chest. She hadn't thought of that way.

"Thank you," she murmured into his chest. "I don't know what I would have done if you didn't show up when you did. I've never been that frightened before.... I kept trying but I couldn't reach him, and I couldn't even get him to talk to me,"--the sobs were breaking up her words. "That little boy is my life."

Logan gently rocked her, smoothed her hair, and held her tight.

Andres let out a deep breath and ruffled the back of his hair as he crossed the threshold into the waiting room. His mother, Elena, was only a step behind him.

His feet locked in place when he glanced up and it looked as though his best friend and his sister were in an embrace. "You aren't seriously hitting on my sister right now, are you?" Andres' shoulders squared off, and he took a step closer. "Do you realize the day she's had?"

Logan looked up and shook his head no and then went back to cradling Izzy.

"Oh, shush, he's not hitting on her," Elena's brow furrowed, "they're together."

"What? In a relationship? Logan is dating my sister?" Andres pulled his chin back and his eyes went between the couple and his mom.

Elena wagged her finger softly. "You get no say in this. You can't keep him all to yourself. Your sister deserves someone like Logan. He'll take care of her. He just proved that."

Izzy's head lifted at her mother's words. The simple acknowledgment melted over her chest like warm honey in tea. She looked up at Logan and could see the softening of his eyes, the strands of blue shining through the ocean of gray. He traced his finger along the edge of her cheek. She tightened her hold around his waist and dropped her head back to his chest. His lips brushed the top of her head and she relished that they finally both knew where they stood.

"Isabella Morales, I'm in love with you and I'll shout it from the rooftops. I won't let anyone stand in our way."

"Logan Roberts, I feel the same way."

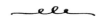

I value each of my readers and look forward to
getting to know you more.
Let's connect on Instagram
http://www.instagram.com/AuthorAveryLawrence
or Facebook
http://www.facebook.com/AuthorAvery/
and sign up here—
http://storyteller.ck.page/0df2fb67a9
this will keep you up to date on
Rose River releases, fun giveaways, and
all things sweet romance.

ele

What are your favorite things? Mine are writing, snickerdoodle cookies, the ocean, and dark chocolate; not necessarily in that order. Writing is something I've always enjoyed. I even have a stack of journals I kept through college that I can't decide if I should burn... or mine for material! In junior high, I even wrote a Christmas play; filled with themes of love and redemption. Themes I still enjoy today.

It's been a wild ride, but I've finally found my own happily ever after. Part of finding this happy place has also meant my world has shifted in a way that space has opened up to write.

So here I am—authentically writing (fictitiously) for your enjoyment. My goal is to create a world that warms the heart and lets you get swept away.

Life is hard; we all need that.

Rose River, where the cowboys still have ranches, the ocean isn't too far away, and love is always the order of the day.

Look for

Rain from the River

Book 2 in the Rose River Romance Series

Coming Summer 2022

Made in United States
North Haven, CT
18 October 2022

25591838R10138